I0570651

GOODNIGHT KISSES

WILD CANYON ESTATES STORIES, #1

TE SHERIDAN

Goodnight Kisses

Wild Canyon Estates Stories

by

TE Sheridan

Contemporary Romance Novella

Published by TE Sheridan

Edited by A. Marie

Cover Photo: Deposit Photos

Cover Design by Redbird Designs

All Rights Reserved

Copyright © 2019 by TE Sheridan

ISBN#: 978-09847245-9-8

Names, characters, and incidents depicted in this book are products of the author's imagination or are used fictitiously. Any resemblance to actual events, or person, living or dead, is coincidental and not the intent of the author.

No part of this book may be reproduced in any form or by any electronic or mechanical means, including information storage and retrieval systems, without written permission from the author, except for the use of brief quotations in a book review.

1

Leslie Brewer stretched and leaned sideways to get a better look at the thunderclouds rolling low over the building. The sky above was a threatening shade of gray; in the distance, the gray darkened to nearly black. She shivered with anticipation and then turned back to her desk. She loved a good storm. Just hoped she could make it home before things got dicey out there. As much as she loved to sit at home and listen to the rain and thunder, she wasn't crazy about navigating her little Rav 4 through streets flooded badly enough to look like canals.

The forecast was calling for enough rain that Leslie had considered buying a Jon boat this morning to drive home tonight. She flopped back in her chair and eyed the clock on the wall. The minute hand hovered and then moved and then hovered: 4:37ish. She yawned, moved her eyes to the digital time stamp in the corner of her computer screen. 4:39.

Okay, she could handle twenty-one minutes. Even if it did start raining, and really, the rain still appeared to be a few miles out.

"Brewer!"

A bright green stress ball flew at her as Jace Hardin walked into the front office and retail space. She lifted a lazy hand to catch it and gave him a look that asked if that was all the better he could do.

"Really?" she asked with a small grin. She turned the ball over in her hands and read the black print out loud. "Hardin Landscaping." She lifted only her eyes to look at Jace, drank in the early summer tan and the thick-fringed lashes around his eyes before he realized she was looking at him. "Stress balls?"

Head bent over a broken lawn mower belt, he grinned without looking at her.

"I know." He shrugged apologetically. "I think Dad let the grandkids help with the marketing stuff this month."

Leslie rolled her eyes. "Please. Which of your nieces and nephews would you have me believe wanted *stress* balls?"

Still without really looking at her, Jace snorted and laughed softly. There were seven of them, four boys and three girls, and from what Leslie knew, the girls were almost better athletes than the boys. The employees at Hardin always teased the brothers (Jace, Adam, and Brendon) to add two more so they could just field a team out at Bennett Park. Jace, being the youngest and most newly-wed, took the brunt of the teasing. Leslie had lost track of the times she'd heard someone ask him when he and Erin were going to add to the Hardin brood.

Leslie wondered if he got tired of hearing it. God knows, she did, and she was just an employee. Okay, a friend of the family, good friend to Jace—they'd gone to school together—and she loved the whole bunch of Hardins. But she wondered if Jace and Erin felt pressured about the baby thing.

Not your business, she reminded herself.

Jace finally looked up and crossed the office to her desk.

"Got a number?"

"Yeah. We're outta them out back." He handed her the broken belt, index finger on the small number printed in white on the outside of the belt. Leslie was careful not to let her eyes linger on the gold band on his ring finger. "Guess I coulda just ordered one from the back room—"

"But you had to come up and see my smiling face," she interrupted him as she took the belt. She set it on her desk, ignored the way it sort of looked like a snake there, ready to strike her, and wrapped her fingers around her mouse to do an online search.

"That's exactly right," Jace agreed, but he sounded distracted. She shot him a quick look and saw that he was leaning over her desk, hands braced on her calendar, looking out the window. "Erin's going out tonight."

She knew him well enough to know he was worried about his wife.

"What time?"

"Seven, I think."

"Storm should be over by then," she reminded him.

She typed the part number into the search box on her order form.

"I know." He nodded. Stood up straight. Picked up the stress ball and gave it a squeeze. He caught her looking at him, and they shared a grin. "Did you hear Marcus pitched a one-hitter last night?"

"Did I hear?" She laughed softly. "It's all your dad has talked about all day."

Jace shrugged when she glanced at him.

"Proud grandpa."

"Yeah, I've noticed that. How many of these do you need?"

"Get me five," he answered. "Big plans tonight?"

"Mmm. You know it. Me and a glass of wine and a big fat book."

"I thought you were the storm chaser."

Leslie finished the part order and closed out of the website.

"Go out chasing a tornado one time, and you get a reputation—"

"I think it was more than once."

"I think you were there, too."

Jace laughed and shook his head.

"Seriously? No date?"

"No date." She shrugged. Used to be, they talked about this stuff easily. Maybe not terribly often, but easily enough. She and Jace had been close enough to talk about anything back in the day. Before Erin.

"Have you met—"

"Don't even think you're gonna set me up, Jace Hardin." She stood up. "I'm in the middle of a good book, and I can hear the wine calling me now."

"I don't doubt that," he mumbled.

"What's Erin doing tonight?" she asked him. She wandered away from her desk. Felt good to move; she was stiff from sitting for too long.

"I dunno." He set the stress ball down again. "Some makeup party or something."

"Kinda weird for a Friday."

"No kidding," he agreed. "Keely's supposed to have a game tonight, but…" He shot another look toward the window.

Tough as nails, Keely Hardin was the oldest of his nieces, the second oldest of all of them, and she was currently holding a batting average near five hundred.

"Eh." Leslie turned her nose up. "I hope she doesn't get rained out."

"I think it's a given," he answered, nodding at the window again. Leslie raised her eyebrows as the first raindrops hit the glass. "Wanna go?"

"To a rained-out game?" she asked with a grin.

"If they play?"

"No. Thanks." She shook her head.

"Must be a good book."

"I'm saying." She nodded. She popped her neck, rolled her shoulders, and then made her way back to the desk. Reached to grab her purse from the bottom drawer. Jace moved to the front door of the office and stood watching the rain as the storm gained momentum. She took the opportunity to study him as she pulled her phone from her purse.

Khaki carpenter shorts. Royal blue Hardin Landscaping t-shirt. Tan legs tucked into beat up brown boots. He was easy on the eyes, always had been. He'd kissed her once. On her sixteenth birthday. As many times as she'd imagined what that kiss would be like, the real thing hadn't quite lived up to her hopes. Apparently, he'd agreed with her. They'd tried. They'd really tried that night, but his tongue in her mouth hadn't done anything for her, and she reminded herself of that often now that he was married, and she still sampled the views every day.

"What?" he asked when she snorted a little laugh. She looked at her phone, shook her head when she felt him looking at her. She had a text from her other best friend, Whitney Oliver.

Come by tonight before you go home.

With another yawn, Leslie texted back to ask her why.

Be my date tonight? Please? Pretty please?

For what?

"Whitney?" Jace asked from the door.

"Yep. Wants me to be her date tonight."

"I bet you tell *her* yes." He turned sideways at the door and propped a shoulder on the steel frame. Leslie shrugged. She couldn't tell him she'd rather just stay home, period. And that if she *had* to go out with Whitney or Jace, she'd choose Whitney. Just because Whitney didn't have a pretty little wife who pretended to like her but sort of appeared nervous or jealous around her.

"She hasn't said what she needs a date for," she mumbled. Phone in hand, she glanced at her computer.

"Shut it down," Jace told her with a nod and a shrug. She moved her mouse again, but this time she clicked on the power option.

Couples shower for a friend from work.

Nope. I don't do showers.

Pretty please? I'll owe you one.

Ten.

Okay. Ten. Pretty please? Please be my date? I'll even buy you dinner.

Leslie laughed out loud, handed Jace her phone when he sauntered back over to her desk.

"Well, if she owes you ten and she's going to buy you dinner, I think you should go."

"Yeah, but what if she expects me to put out?"

"I can tell her that's not gonna happen." He dropped her phone to her desk.

"Hey!" She lunged across the desk and slapped at his hand. "You weren't interested!"

"You didn't let me get far enough to know." He grabbed her hand. "Go out with Whitney. Have some fun for a change."

"I resent that," she said with a grin. "I like being alone."

"Maybe you'll meet someone at the shower—"

"Oh my God!" She rolled her eyes. "Stop it! I'll go with Whitney, but just stop it!"

She sent a quick text in reply to Whitney.

I'll go, but you should know I'm REALLY HUNGRY.

2

"If I'd have known that buying me dinner meant tossing me a snack size bag of corn chips, I think I'd have said no."

Whitney laughed, but she sort of winced, too, and Leslie knew she felt guilty.

"I swear I thought the invitation said seven. I thought we had plenty of time."

"I don't even like corn chips," Leslie announced as she opened the bag and reached in for a handful.

"You do, too!" Whitney argued, but she offered Leslie the bag of potato chips she was holding. Leslie shook her head. "After the shower. I promise. I'll even spring for drinks."

Leslie laughed and shook her head.

"Who's the shower for?"

"Felicia and Matt."

"Oh, yeah." Leslie nodded. "Because I know who the hell Felicia and Matt are."

Whitney giggled quietly. "Felicia Vandiver. She works in bookkeeping. Her fiancé is an EMT or something."

"Am I dressed okay?" Leslie asked with a frown. Working

in a landscaping business, she wore jeans or shorts five days a week. Today was a jeans day, but she was wearing her Hardin t-shirt. Not something she wanted to actually socialize in.

"Mm." Whitney bit her lip. "Wanna borrow a different shirt?"

"Yep."

Whitney led Leslie out of the kitchen and down the short hall to her bedroom.

"Where's Shawn? Why isn't he your date tonight?"

"We broke up." Whitney was so calm as she pulled her closet door open, Leslie thought she'd heard her wrong. Chips still in hand, Whitney used her free hand to browse the tops in her closet. Twice, she looked back at Leslie with a look of concentration and then vetoed whatever she'd been considering.

"Why are you eyeballing me like that?" Leslie asked her. "And what do you mean, you broke up?"

"Because orange isn't your color." Whitney pulled the tail of an orange blouse out to see it better. She studied it a moment and then shivered. "Not mine either. Why did I buy that?"

"Whit?"

Whitney sighed and turned to look at Leslie.

"We got in a huge fight a couple nights ago. And he was on his way to Texas—"

"What the hell's in Texas?"

"He was meeting his brother and a few other guys down there for a baseball game. Guys' weekend."

"What were you fighting about?"

Whitney moved toward the bed and set the bag of chips on the nightstand. "Well, it started with a fight about a girl."

"What girl?" Leslie perched on the edge of Whitney's bed.

"This girl he works with. She's new at the office. She's

like…an intern or something. So, she's doing all the shit jobs. Like getting guys like Shawn coffee every morning."

"And?" Leslie lifted a shoulder and waited for Whitney to go on.

"Well, she's cute. And she's apparently pretty into him."

"Maybe he just said she is."

"I've seen it." Whitney rolled her eyes. "She touches him every chance she gets." She ducked back into the closet again. Leslie held in a sigh. She'd hoped she could get Whitney talking enough that she'd forget the shower. Leslie had sworn off bridal showers after the seventh girl in their class got married within the last two years. She assumed Whitney felt differently about them, as she'd been dating Shawn for several years. "And by touching him, I mean rubbing up against him. She might as well serve 'em up on a tray with his coffee."

Leslie snorted. She sat up straight and did her best to look upset for Whitney when her friend turned back to look at her.

"What?"

"So, a college kid has a thing for him." Leslie shrugged. "Shawn loves you."

Whitney considered Leslie's words for a moment and nodded. "I know. It snowballed. He decided maybe we needed a break."

"And you let him go? To Texas? On a guys' weekend?"

"How was I supposed to stop him?"

Leslie raised her eyebrows. Whitney turned back to the closet for a second and pulled a hanger out.

"Here." She handed the pale blue sleeveless blouse to Leslie. "Try that. It'll probably look better on you than me."

Blue-eyed and blond, Whitney wore a red tank with jeans and black-heeled sandals.

Leslie stood up and pulled her t-shirt off. Slipped the blouse on and smoothed it down over her stomach.

"Okay?" She looked up at Whitney.

"Yep." Whitney squatted down and reached into her closet for a pair of sandals. "Here. Try these."

"This is why I swore off all this crap," Leslie grumbled as she stepped out of her flip flops. She decided it was a good thing she had a fresh pedicure, or Whitney might decide to give her one. "Too much trouble."

"Nuh-uh." Whitney eyed the nude-colored sandals and nodded her approval. "Damn. You look hot." She met Leslie's eyes and grinned. "You swore off this crap because you were sick of buying other people wedding gifts when you had no prospects."

Leslie laughed. She slipped into Whitney's master bathroom to check her hair. She wore it short and mussed, and she had to admit it looked about the same now as it had this morning when she'd left for work. Thankfully, it hadn't been raining too hard when she'd run to the Rav 4 just after five to drive over here.

Whitney picked up the bag of chips from the nightstand and pulled out a few. Leslie pulled the top bathroom drawer open and grabbed Whitney's toothpaste.

"You don't seem very upset about Shawn," she said quietly as she squeezed toothpaste on her finger.

Whitney stuffed the chips in her mouth and then folded the top of the bag over.

"I cried a few buckets when he stormed out of here," she admitted, mouth full of food. Dropped the bag again and joined Leslie at the sink. Leslie handed her the toothpaste and then leaned over to rub some over her teeth.

"Why didn't you call me?" She watched Whitney squeeze some paste onto her toothbrush and then turn the faucet on for a minute to get it wet.

"I dunno." Whitney shrugged. "It was after two in the morning when I finally settled down enough that you could have understood anything I said."

"And? Why didn't you call me?"

"Didn't wanna bother you," Whitney said quietly. She leaned over and stuck her brush in her mouth. "Don't spit on me."

They'd been friends long enough that they'd done this routine more than a time or two. Or ten. Maybe twenty.

"Bother me," Leslie repeated. "You didn't wanna bother me."

"I just…figure you get tired of me whining about me and Shawn. I mean, how many times can I say to you that I wanna get married, and he doesn't, and—"

"You can say it to me however many times you need to." Leslie rubbed her finger over her tongue and then waited for Whitney to move back out of her way before spitting. "You know that."

Leslie cupped her hand under the water and then drank from it to rinse her mouth out.

"I think we'll work it out," Whitney said quietly.

"But?" Leslie patted her mouth dry with the hand towel and then watched Whitney finish brushing and rinse her mouth out. She handed the towel to her and rested her hip against the counter.

"I don't know. Work it out for what?" Whitney put her toothbrush back in the holder and then hung the towel on the rack. "What if I'm wasting my time?"

"You've been in love with Shawn for as long as I can remember."

Whitney nodded and led Leslie back out of the bathroom and through the bedroom and hall to the kitchen. "I have. But that's just it. Years. And nothing's changed. He doesn't even want to live with me, let alone get married."

Leslie watched Whitney fold the top over on the snack bag of corn chips and then clip it with a clothespin. She looked around, realized she left the other chips in the bedroom and jogged back through the hall.

"You don't need to hurry," Leslie mumbled.

"Ah, but this will be fun," Whitney told her when she came back to the kitchen. Leslie offered her a fake smile when she looked at her. "You didn't think I heard that, did you?"

"We could go get some nachos instead."

"I wanna go," Whitney admitted. "I know you don't know them, but Felicia's pretty cool. I think it'll be fun."

"Yeah, yeah." Leslie nodded. "Did you get a gift?"

"I did. It's already in the car."

"Awesome." Leslie followed Whitney down the short hall to the back door.

"Jace got that wife of his pregnant yet?" Whitney asked as they both settled in her Jetta.

"Not you, too." Leslie shook her head.

"What do you mean?" Whitney hit the garage door opener, eyes on the rearview mirror, and slowly backed out. Clear of the garage, she pushed the button again to close the door and zipped out of the drive.

"Erin and Jace are the talk of the office," Leslie mumbled. "Babies, babies, babies. God, the guy's probably got an issue with performance by now with all the discussion going on."

Whitney burst out laughing and rolled her eyes.

"You still got a thing for him?"

She rolled to a stop at the four way on Curry and Juniper and shot Leslie a wink. She was teasing, and Leslie knew it, but she wasn't in the mood for it.

"Whit, kissing him was like kissing…I don't even know. Just…like you think you're about to have some Dove chocolate and you take a big bite and it's that generic stuff your great aunt puts in a little plastic Easter basket for you when you're ten."

"Kissing Jace is like eating generic chocolate?"

"Yeah?" Leslie tossed her hands up helplessly. "Yeah. I mean…I wanted to like it, but I didn't. Didn't hate it. Didn't love it."

"I know, I know." Whitney nodded. "So hard to believe, though. He's so cute."

Cute was not the word Leslie would use to describe Jace Hardin, but she nodded in agreement anyway.

"What about Topher Groll?"

Leslie blinked and cocked her head to stare at Whitney.

"What about him?"

"You made out with him."

"Once."

"And it was pretty hot?"

"Definitely not generic chocolate," Leslie mumbled.

"He's single," Whitney told her. "Saw him at the bank the other day. He was there for a meeting with someone. Heard him say something about his ex-wife."

"First?" Leslie shook her head. "I don't want someone else's ex-husband. There's a reason he's divorced—"

"Yeah, maybe his wife cheated."

"And second?" Leslie punched Whitney playfully in the arm. "Stop it. I am not so pathetic that I can't get a date."

"No, you're just impossible to satisfy."

"I have high standards." Leslie rested her head on her seat. "Where is this shower?"

"Wild Canyon Estates," Whitney answered. She glanced at Leslie as she slowed at the stoplight at Melbourne. "And do I not have high standards? Is that what you're saying?"

"No. But all the good guys are taken."

Suddenly the rain went from a sprinkle to a heavy downpour. Leslie sighed and groaned out loud.

"Well, Keely's definitely gonna be rained out now," she mumbled.

"What?"

"Nothing."

"Les?"

"Hmm?"

"This is gonna be fun tonight. Just…" She shrugged. "Have fun. Okay?"

"Are you telling me to hook up with someone?"

"Um…" Whitney pursed her lips and then slowed at the entrance to Wild Canyon Estates. "Yeah, I guess I am."

"Serial killer movies start out like this, you know?"

"Yeah, but serial killers only go for women who wear no bra or whose bra matches their underwear."

"You didn't see my underwear."

"No, but I hope it doesn't match, because your bra looked too matronly."

"It's lace."

"Yeah, but it might as well be a turtleneck for all it showed."

"So." Leslie looked around as Whitney pulled the Jetta to the curb behind a long line of other cars. "That ten that you owe me…"

Whitney arched her eyebrows. "You're gonna stick it to me, aren't you?"

"You bet your ass I am." Leslie grinned.

They sat for a moment until the rain slackened from heavy downpour to steady. Then they climbed from the car and ran together, laughing, up to the front porch.

"Have I mentioned I hate rain?" Whitney asked as she pressed the doorbell.

"Have I mentioned I hate wedding showers?"

Whitney chuckled. "You don't need to specify, ya know?"

"What?"

"Showers. You hate showers. Period."

"Not true. I love steamy showers when shared with the right—"

The door opened, and a bald guy with shoulders like an NFL defensive lineman grinned and threw his hands in the air when he saw Whitney.

"Whitney!"

"Hey, Frank." Whitney hugged him and then turned to Leslie. "This is my date tonight. Leslie Brewer, this is Frank Jackson. He works in the mortgage department at the bank."

"Leslie." Frank toned the grin down and offered her his hand for a shake. "Nice to meet you."

"Hi, Frank." Leslie shook his hand.

"Les and I went to school together," Whitney announced. "And Shawn's out of town."

Leslie was glad to have heard the story Whitney would use for the evening, though she had no intention of sharing it with anyone, anyway. They'd get back together, eventually.

"Any friend of Whitney's is a friend of ours." Frank backed up and gestured for them to come inside. "C'mon. Let's get you two hooked up. Passports are this way."

Whitney glanced at Leslie with a suspicious frown.

"Passports?" she mouthed.

"Your party," Leslie mouthed back with a shrug.

3

"Hey! Whitney!"

Leslie looked at her again and arched her eyebrows as if to repeat what she'd just said. Whitney looked at her with big eyes, shrugged, and then turned to the woman at the table in the elegant entryway. Leslie took stock of the marble flooring and the ornate lamp at the far end of the table. The woman's low-cut blouse. Not even admitted to the party yet, and she was ready to run.

"Donna!" Whitney's smile was big and real, but she wasn't as comfortable with this woman as she'd been with Frank.

"I'm so glad you could come." The other woman kissed Whitney's cheek and then looked at Leslie. "I'm Donna. Frank's wife."

"Donna and I worked together. She left the bank last year. Traded us in for all new coworkers and a different bank," Whitney told Leslie. "Donna, this is my friend Leslie."

"Hi, Leslie." Donna, a few years on them but still vivacious and bubbly and very attractive, reached a hand out and skimmed her blood red fingernails down Leslie's arm. "Okay. Let's get you girls set up with a passport."

"Donna?" Whitney dragged her eyes from Leslie to the other woman, who was now bent over the table. They watched her select two big green index cards. There was something printed on the cards, but Leslie couldn't make anything out from where she stood.

"Hmm?" The woman straightened and offered Whitney another smile.

"Why do we need passports?"

Leslie felt a ripple of nerves thread through her belly at Whitney's friend's low, sultry laugh.

"Well, for the games, hon."

Whitney nodded as Donna handed a card first to her and then to Leslie. Whitney glanced at the card and then looked at Leslie with wide eyes and a mix of panic and guilt written on her face.

"This is an adult night," Donna told them. "We're playing adult games."

"What does that mean?" Leslie asked quietly. Maybe the woman—Donna—meant something as harmless (still embarrassing) as *Dirty Word Scrabble* or even *Dirty Pictures.* Whitney laughed softly.

"You're kidding. Right?" Whitney asked. She looked from Leslie back to her passport.

"Nope." Donna picked up a couple of white poker chips. "Ready?"

"Um." Whitney shook her head. Leslie held the card up and read the first line. *Dirty Word Scrabble*. Okay. Wasn't her favorite thing to do with strangers, but maybe if she drank a beer or two, she'd be okay. Maybe it would even be fun. "No?"

"Here's how it works." Donna stepped around the table and took Whitney's passport. "There are a total of six games. Each game you play, you get a stamp on your passport."

She looked from Whitney to Leslie and continued when they both nodded.

"You have to participate in five of the six games to qualify."

"Qualify for what?"

"A five-hundred-dollar gift card for dinner at Oakley's Grill."

"Wow." Whitney laughed, but Leslie heard the nerves in the note.

"And also." Donna held a hand up to get their attention.

"What?"

"Everyone gets a poker chip. By the time you leave, choose someone you want to kiss goodnight. The person with the most poker chips at the end of the night gets his or her own special prize."

"Kiss…someone…goodnight…" Whitney blew out a quick huff. "Donna, Shawn would have—"

"Sweetheart, I don't know why, but you aren't with Shawn right now." Donna winked. "These are adult games. Kissing someone goodnight is the least of it."

"What does that mean?"

"There're a lot of couples here together. A lot of married couples." Donna shrugged and smiled. "But anything goes. It's one night. One night of anything-goes fun. No harm done."

The doorbell rang. Leslie stared at Whitney as Donna plopped the poker chips in their hands and wandered away from them to answer the door. Frank was nowhere in sight.

"You know that ten you owe me?" Leslie mumbled.

"Oh, God." Whitney laughed nervously again. "No kidding."

"She didn't say if there's a penalty if you still have your chip at the end of the night."

Whitney took a deep breath.

"So. Let's get a drink."

"Better idea." Leslie wiggled her eyebrows. "Let's get the hell out of here."

Whitney narrowed her eyes at her and stared silently.

"What?" Leslie looked down at herself. At the blouse she'd borrowed from Whitney. She couldn't possibly have spilled anything on it, unless Whitney saw toothpaste on it somewhere.

"Aren't you even the slightest bit curious?"

Leslie looked around the entrance way and again noticed the marble flooring and the honey blonde woodwork. Hell, she was curious about the house. Who knew what to think about the party?

"Kind of," she admitted.

"We could check it out," Whitney suggested. "Get out whenever we want."

Leslie borrowed the low, sultry laugh Donna had used on them a few minutes ago.

"Do we need a code word?"

"How about *baby*?"

"Ew. No." Leslie shivered. "How about *stress*?"

"Too obvious." Whitney shook her head. "*Iguana.*"

"How in the hell do you work *iguana* into a conversation?" Leslie asked, but Whitney grabbed her hand and yanked her through the entryway to a big open kitchen and living area. Leslie was too taken with the marble floor the color of sand and the honey blonde cabinetry in the kitchen to argue. People milled about everywhere, crowded around a big table in a nook off the kitchen and another table set up in the middle of the big open room. The house was well-lit and seemingly too perfect to breathe in.

Whitney dragged her past the table in the middle of the room where six people appeared to be playing *Dirty Pictures*. Leslie caught a glimpse of a drawing she suspected was supposed to be hard-on or maybe just hard, though really, it looked like a stick arrow. She listened to the guesses as Whitney pulled her past the table, and then suddenly, she and Whitney were outside on a large cobblestone patio, bellied up to a portable bar. There were people out here, too. Didn't appear to be any games going on, as it was raining. But there was a tent over the bar, and three people in a swimming pool. Leslie almost tugged on Whitney's arm to point out that people here were swimming when it was raining, but before she could open her mouth, she realized all three of them—two men and one woman—were naked in the water.

"Damn." She cleared her throat. "I'm gonna need something really strong."

Whitney shot her a frown, turned to the bartender, and asked what he had. The guy—older, but still easy on the eyes—told Whitney to name it, he had it.

"Appletini?" she glanced at Leslie.

"Sure."

"How about a chocolate raspberry martini?" the guy suggested.

"I'll go with that," Leslie agreed. Whitney shrugged and nodded.

"And I'm gonna suggest you both start with a shot."

"I don't do shots—"

He interrupted Whitney with a smile. "If you've never been to one of Donna and Frank's parties before, I suggest a shot."

"We'll take a shot." Leslie rested an elbow on the bar. The bartender winked and nodded. When he turned his back to them, Leslie nodded backwards to the pool.

"Oh." Whitney's face froze in a mask of surprise when she saw the nude woman climb from the water. "She looks cold."

"Okay." The guy turned back to them with two shot

glasses in hand. "I'm giving you both Screaming Blue Vikings. Trust me. Easy to swallow."

"Really?" Leslie asked as she picked up her glass. "It'll be the first thing here that is."

He chuckled. Whitney picked up her glass and stared at it suspiciously.

"I haven't done shots since that one night three years ago."

Leslie nodded. She remembered the night well. It had ended with Whitney getting sick in the back of her old car.

"Play the games," the guy told them. "It's a fun night. And everyone here is very discreet."

Leslie took a deep breath and blinked at him. She lifted the shot and tossed it back quickly. Whitney still stood with hers in hand, eyes moving from the blue liquor to Leslie.

"Do it," Leslie ordered her.

"You'll play? You'll do this?" Whitney asked quietly.

Leslie shrugged one shoulder helplessly.

"If you do."

Whitney stared at her a moment longer. "You think Shawn's…"

Leslie shook her head. "I don't know. But you broke up, or you're on a break or something. I'm not gonna tell him."

Whitney sighed and threw the shot back. She twitched a bit as she swallowed, but she licked her lips and glanced at the bartender.

"Okay."

"Here ya go." He handed them their drinks and gave them both a big smile.

"Are these people made of money?" Leslie asked Whitney as they wandered away from the bar, heads tipped together.

"Yes," Whitney answered. "What do you wanna play first?"

"Um." Leslie looked down at her passport. "I have no idea. It's like what's the least…"

"Yeah. I don't even know." Whitney glanced at her passport and then looked around. "Oh! There's Felicia."

"Who?"

"The bride-to-be," Whitney reminded her. "Let's go see what she's doing."

Leslie looked up and followed Whitney's gaze. She noticed a petite dark-haired girl sitting in a circle on the floor behind the table in the middle of the room.

"Felicia!" Whitney hollered. Leslie saw the clear glass bottle in the center of the circle as the bride-to-be, who wore a cute little tiara with a piece of white tulle attached, turned to see who was hollering at her.

"Hey, Whit!" The girl jumped up gracefully from the floor to hug Whitney. Leslie stood behind them awkwardly. She was a little bit afraid to look around, after seeing so much skin out in the pool. She did, though, carefully. There was music pumping in the background, just loud enough to feel the beat but not so much that it distracted her. She watched people at the table, a few of them scribbling away on their scratch pads. Noticed a few couples dancing. Thank God that wasn't on the passport. Leslie was a self-conscious dancer in the most mundane circumstances. Everyone seemed relaxed, which told her this was a group that apparently partied together—like this—often.

"Les."

Whitney tugged at her hand as her eyes locked with a tall guy behind the kitchen counter. His gray shirt sculpted delicious-looking shoulders. His dark hair was tied back in a short ponytail.

He smiled, and Leslie resisted the urge to look over her shoulder to see if anyone was standing there behind her. From this distance, she couldn't see his eyes well enough to decide if they were blue or gray, but they were certainly intense on her. Heat simmered low in her belly as he continued to watch her with a sharp, hungry gaze.

"Leslie."

"Hmm?" She turned to Whitney.

"This is Felicia. Felicia, this is my friend Leslie."

Leslie wanted to look back at the guy at the counter, but she remembered her manners and offered a friendly hello to the bride-to-be.

"You're just in time." Felicia nodded to the group of people sitting on the floor. "Just getting ready to start *Spin the Bottle*."

"Um." Leslie raised her eyebrows and licked her lips. Whitney squeezed her fingers and then let go of her hand.

"So, the rules," Felicia started, "as I've been told…anything goes. You spin the bottle. You roll a die. Only one, two, and three count. You roll a four or up, and you lose a turn."

Whitney nodded slowly. "What does anything goes mean?"

"What're we rolling the die for?" Leslie asked her.

"One minute. Two minutes. Three minutes." Felicia shrugged and rattled off a carefree laugh. "In the middle of the circle. And anything goes. You can talk to whoever you're with. You can kiss him or her. Or whatever you wanna do."

"Oh, man." Leslie groaned.

"Is Matt—"

"They split us up." Felicia shook her head. "Right now, he's playing strip poker."

Leslie held her breath. Felicia leaned forward to whisper to them.

"See that guy? In the pink shirt?" She nodded her head to a dark-haired guy across the circle. "I'm hoping I get at least two minutes with him."

Whitney laughed softly.

"I know." Felicia nodded. "Kind of weird. But I'd rather do

this…" She swung her hands around to include the whole party, Leslie assumed, "than me and the girls going to the bar for a drink and Matt's guys taking him to a strip joint and buying him lap dances all night."

"Really?" Whitney asked her. "Felicia, there're three people skinny-dipping out in the pool. They weren't doing laps."

Felicia grinned. "Yeah, but I could be the next one out in the pool, right? Isn't that fair?"

Whitney shrugged and sort of nodded as Felicia went back to the circle.

"Just think." Leslie leaned into Whitney. "If you and Shawn do get married, Donna and Frank will throw your shower."

"Don't you dare let that happen, Leslie Brewer!"

Whitney took Leslie's hand and pulled her to the circle. They crowded in between two guys and sat down. Leslie took a healthy sip of her martini.

"Hey." Felicia grabbed the bottle and handed it to Whitney. "You can start."

"No, hey, it's—"

"How's it going over here?" Frank's voice boomed over them. Leslie looked first at Whitney and then Frank. She studied him for a moment, guessed him to be in his fifties. Seemed nice. Just struck her as odd that he and his wife were hosting what seemed to translate as a giant orgy. If not odd, certainly out of her league. "Whitney's starting? Great. Go for it, Whit."

"Yeah, go for it, Whit." Leslie flashed a big grin at her. Whitney bit back a groan, set the bottle down, and gave it a spin. Leslie felt the blood drain from her face when it stopped, pointed at her.

4

"Are you freaking kidding me?" She ducked her chin and shook her head.

"Okay." The guy next to Whitney plopped the die in her hand. Leslie prayed for a one. Anything more might be excruciating. Whitney set her drink down and wiped her palms on her jeans. Leslie watched her roll the die. She managed to keep her sigh of relief quiet when the cube stopped with only one black spot facing up.

"Whitney and Leslie for a minute," Frank announced.

"I hope he's not going to do play by play," Leslie groaned as she set her drink back behind Whitney.

"Might get bored," Whitney decided. "It took me ten minutes to work up the nerve to kiss someone the first time I played *Spin the Bottle*."

"Yeah, you were twelve," Leslie reminded her.

The two of them scooched into the center of the circle. Leslie stared at Whitney and shook her head. "Yeah, this'll be fun." She nodded. "Isn't that what you said?"

"Shut up." Whitney laughed. "Is there a timer going?"

"Ready to start?" Frank asked.

"Hell, yes." Whitney nodded.

Someone in the circle cut loose with a big whistle. Someone across the room chanted what sounded like *shirt*, so Leslie assumed someone had just lost his or her shirt in strip poker.

"Maybe we shoulda done a few shots." Whitney arched her eyebrows.

"Mighta helped," Leslie agreed.

Whitney lifted her hand. Leslie assumed when she reached for her that she'd yank her hair and drop a quick kiss on her cheek, but someone in the circle hollered for tongue. Leslie felt her cheeks light with fire.

"You gonna forgive me for this?" Whitney curled her fingers around the back of Leslie's neck.

"I haven't decided." Leslie shrugged. "I guess it depends on how good you kiss."

"This is—"

"And time's ticking." Leslie winked at her and then laughed.

"I'm scared you're gonna lump me in with Jace."

Leslie shook her head, but she stilled when Whitney leaned in close to her and brushed her lips over hers. Assuming that was it, Leslie almost drew back from her, but Whitney urged her closer with her hand. Leslie gasped in surprise, and then suddenly, Whitney's tongue traced over her lips.

"You're really doing this," Leslie whispered. They grinned, lips pressed together again.

"I don't play anything half-heartedly." Whitney's free hand cupped her chin. "C'mon. Wow me."

"Is that a dare?" Leslie drew back and laughed.

Whitney shrugged and arched her eyebrows.

This time, when Whitney's tongue touched her lips, Leslie opened her mouth and breathed slowly, deeply. When

Whitney slid her tongue between her lips, Leslie sucked on it and then rubbed it with her own. She tasted the shot and the chocolate martini, and Whitney's tongue explored her mouth tenderly. Whitney broke the kiss to gasp for a quick breath, and Leslie found herself reaching for her. Fingers in her long hair, she kissed her, eagerly exploring Whitney's mouth with her tongue.

"Time," Frank announced.

They drew apart, both of them laughing, though Leslie wasn't sure she was amused. A little bit embarrassed that this group of strangers had watched her kiss her best friend. A little bit aroused, because of the liquor and the atmosphere and the fact that someone had just kissed her so intimately.

They scooted back to the circle, but Leslie dropped her head back and sighed when she remembered it was her turn to spin the bottle now. She eyed Whitney as she reached for it.

"I still haven't decided if I'm going to forgive you for dragging me here."

Whitney only laughed as Leslie gave the bottle a quick spin. She hesitated to look up when it stopped. Found that it was pointing at a guy across the circle. Close-cropped silver hair, sideburns, and sliver framed glasses. His grin made Leslie laugh. He raised his eyebrows as she reached for the die.

"I gotta tell ya," he called to her, "after watching that little warm up kiss, I'm hoping for a three."

"Hey, I'm a rookie," she reminded him. He laughed. Lifted a glass to sip on something. Leslie noticed a wedding band on his finger. "Damn. First time for a lot of things tonight."

"What?" Whitney turned her head to look at her, but Leslie only shook her head.

She tossed the die. Felt a little stab of nerves when she saw two dots face up.

"I'm Craig," he told her as he moved to the center of the circle.

"And I'm nervous," she answered with a laugh.

"You just kissed a girl. What's to be nervous about?"

"I've known Whit since I was, like, ten."

"We've got two minutes," he reminded her. She nodded and took a deep breath. She felt eyes boring into her everywhere, like little needles.

"Is your wife here?"

"Yep." He nodded. "I think she's in the pool."

"In the pool?" Leslie blinked at him.

"Yep."

"And that's—? Okay?"

"Okay with me."

Leslie glanced at Whitney with wide eyes. Whitney grinned. Took a big swallow of her martini. Leslie wished she'd have done the same. With a quick breath, she turned back to Craig and leaned into him. Again, someone in the circle called for tongue, and Leslie was laughing as she kissed him. He smelled like winter and evergreens, and he tasted like whisky. She wasn't a whisky drinker, but she wasn't turned off by it. He returned her kiss with a little more aggression than she'd shown for Whitney's kiss, but she was surprised to realize she wasn't impressed.

Kissing Whitney had been more intriguing. Not to mention she'd tasted like chocolate.

"So, you did the spinning," he said quietly as she broke the kiss. "Which means everything is your move."

Leslie laughed, but she ducked her head quickly.

"Yeah, I'm not used to an audience," she answered him. "Or making out with strangers."

"Takes some time," he admitted.

"You're totally okay with your wife out there in the pool with two other men?"

"Only here." He nodded.

"Blows me away."

"We've been married thirty years."

Leslie shook her head and sighed again.

"Can I just kiss you again? You gotta let me warm up to this."

He laughed and lifted a shoulder in a lazy shrug. "Anything you want."

"I've only had one drink," she told him. "Kinda feel like I was watching porn and fell asleep and now I'm dreaming this."

He cocked his head and stared at her with an amused look on his face. Leslie was a little bit relieved to hear people in the circle talking quietly. Maybe they were bored watching her. This time, she reached for him, slid her hand around the back of his neck. His skin was warm, and suddenly, she wondered if he'd been out in the pool with someone.

What the hell? He was sexy; she was single. What would it hurt to have a little fun?

She kissed him again, hungry for it now that she'd decided just to go with it. She couldn't remember the last time she'd had sex; it had been at least two months. Maybe three. And that night hadn't been anything to brag about. She most definitely couldn't remember the last time she'd had sex to brag about. Maybe three or four years ago.

This guy was a greedy kisser. His tongue stroked hers and her lips; he nipped at her gently, and Leslie wondered what it would feel like if he touched her. She wasn't quite ready for that, though. Maybe another shot. Or ten. When Frank called their time, she was relieved to move back to her spot by Whitney.

"How was that?" Whitney whispered.

Leslie reached for her drink, surprised to find a fresh

martini in its place. She eyed it carefully, decided she might
need her drinks on speed dial or even IV if she was going to
make it through the night.

"Wet," she told Whitney as she took a healthy drink.

"Better than kissing me?"

When Leslie lifted her eyes from the glass, she saw the
ornery grin on Whitney's face.

"Actually, no."

"Really?" Whitney laughed.

The bottle had been spun and Craig rolled a two. Leslie
and Whitney watched Craig and Felicia move to the center
of the circle.

"Yeah, really," Leslie answered. "I can't believe she's into
this. Kinda weird for getting married."

Whitney nodded. "Say the word and we'll go."

Leslie looked at Whitney, surprised to hear her say so.

"Really? I thought it might be kinda fun."

"You gonna get in on the pool activities?"

"No way." Leslie frowned. "But this seems…sort of fun."

Since Craig spun the bottle, he was in control of this two-
minute session. Leslie saw that he was not only a greedy
kisser, he was handsy. Hands in Felicia's halter top with less
than ten seconds off the clock. Leslie looked around, noticed
some people in the circle watching them. Some were talking.
Others were looking around the house at the other groups.
She wondered how many of them had been to a party here
like this before, and how many of them were rookies like she
and Whitney.

She'd never watched real people make out, just movie
people. Probably helped that everyone here seemed to be
some sort of pretty or sexy, but she found that no matter
how much she looked around, her eyes kept coming back to
whoever was in the center of the circle. After Craig and Felicia, it was Felicia and some girl named Beth. They got three

minutes. Leslie was a little bit stunned when Felicia's hands moved quickly and Beth was suddenly topless.

"Shawn's gonna kill me," Whitney mumbled.

"You haven't done anything."

"I kissed you."

"That doesn't count." Leslie shook her head.

"You said it was better than that guy."

"It was, but it still doesn't count."

Leslie looked over her shoulder. She didn't want to admit it, even to herself, but she was looking for the guy she'd seen at the counter earlier. Disappointed when she didn't see him, she turned around as the next spinner took the bottle. Watched, a little surprised again, when the next couple—a woman who looked a little older and a kid who looked fresh out of high school—went at it with three minutes on the clock.

"I'm not sure I'm into getting naked in the middle of a circle of people," she told Whitney.

"No kidding."

Three minutes was plenty of time for fun. The woman, who had spun the bottle, had her hands all over the kid.

"Shawn and I made a video once." Whitney leaned into her. "It's really weird to watch yourself have sex."

Leslie looked at Whitney curiously.

"How much have you had to drink?"

Whitney laughed softly. "No more than you. Why?"

"You never told me that. I'm assuming it's the alcohol talking."

Whitney shrugged. "We're watching a bank VP give someone's son a hand job. The whole night's surreal."

Leslie answered with a reluctant nod. "Good point. You worried about it?"

"This?" Whitney nodded toward the center of the circle.

"The video."

"Mm." Whitney shrugged. Took a deep breath. "Not really."

"You guys'll work it out."

"I don't know if I want to, Les." This time, Whitney avoided her eyes. "If he doesn't want to get married, maybe it's time I move on. I want more than movie dates and sex on the go."

The kid took his turn with the bottle. Leslie watched with amusement when it stopped on Whitney.

"Have some fun." Leslie nudged her with her knee.

"Well, I know where my hand is not going."

Leslie snorted. She took another quick glance around the room. Still no sexy dark-haired, broad-shouldered guy anywhere to be seen.

Whitney was at this kid's mercy, although Leslie hoped if he pushed for something that Whitney wasn't comfortable with, she would stop him. If watching real people, real strangers make out was weird, watching her best friend with this kid was a strange mix of fun and uncomfortable. The kid didn't push, but Leslie noticed when his hands disappeared, Whitney didn't fight him. She wondered how long the game continued. If it stopped after everyone had a turn, or if you dropped out when you wanted. Didn't seem to be that you had to win a game, just play to get a stamp on your passport.

She looked around again when Whitney spun the bottle. Glimpsed *the guy* near the strip poker table, though he didn't seem to be playing. He was talking to another guy—both of them fully clothed—holding a longneck beer. Leslie looked away quickly; she didn't want him to catch her staring. Well. She kind of did, but the thought made her a little dizzy. She watched Whitney move back to the center of the circle with a muscular blonde. Flicked her eyes back to the hot ponytail guy. When she saw him watching her, her body exploded with heat.

Kissing the guy named Craig was lukewarm compared to making eye contact with this guy. Leslie wanted to ask Whitney if she knew him, but she couldn't now. Whitney was half-straddling the blonde's lap in the center of the circle, and they were both laughing. Leslie wondered what she'd missed.

When the bottle pointed at her again several spins later, Leslie was feeling pretty mellow. Ready to move on. Try her hand at *Dirty Word Scrabble*. Or really, just try her hands with the guy with the sexy shoulders. But she took her turn. He was kind of cute, but he tasted like garlic salt, and Leslie preferred her garlic salt on pasta or pizza. Thankfully, they only had a minute. She suffered through it, whispered with a grin to Whitney that she was still the best kisser in the circle, and then spun the bottle. Decided this would be her last go around, unless leaving early would be frowned upon. Another minute with another subpar kisser. She climbed to her feet as that guy spun the bottle. Whitney looked up at her in askance.

"Will you be okay?" She arched her brows and nodded toward the center of the circle. As far as she could tell, Whitney trusted Frank and Donna, but she didn't want to wander off and leave Whitney alone if she was uncomfortable. When Whitney nodded and waved her away, Leslie mumbled that she needed some air and slipped away from the circle. Suddenly, she wondered if the ponytail guy had watched her kissing people. What would he think of her? But then, why did it matter? She didn't even know him.

She slipped out the French doors in the back, forgetting that the pool was part of the party fun. Hearing the splashes and giggles, she made a sharp right and wandered away from the house. Took a gulp of her martini that had apparently been delivered by some invisible drink waiter. Or her guardian angel, maybe.

She could go back in and tell Whitney she needed to go home and feed her pet iguana. But she wasn't sure she needed to leave. Maybe taking a few minutes to herself out here would be enough. She thought she'd had enough of *Spin the Bottle*, and she had no desire to play strip poker, but she wasn't desperate to leave, either.

She laughed as she wandered the backyard. Was she content to stay because this was by far the most bizarre party she'd ever been to? That she would ever go to in her life? Or was she content to stay because she was buzzing from the martinis and an abundance of skin and sexuality?

Or was she still hoping to run into the guy with the pony-tail and the broad shoulders?

Probably a little of all of the above, if she were being honest. She wasn't invested in winning the gift card at the end of the night. With a grin, she reached into her pocket and closed her fingers around the poker chip. If she could find him, she'd lay a hell of a kiss on him and give him her poker chip.

She laughed softly. What would Jace think? She'd begged off Keely's softball game so she could go home and read. Instead, she'd come out with Whitney, and her mouth had had more action in the last half hour than in the past two or three months.

"I wondered where you'd disappeared to."

At the now open gate at the driveway in front of the house—the rain had stopped, but the streets and grass were wet, and the smell of rain on the pavement comforted her—she turned to look over her shoulder. The *guy*, bottle in hand, approached her with a smile.

"Needed some air." She grinned.

"Not the backyard kind?" He arched an eyebrow sugges-tively. Embarrassed, Leslie looked away quickly.

"No. Just some air."

"This is crazy," he said as if he was agreeing with her, as if she'd said a lot more than what had actually come out of her mouth.

"Yeah. I guess I got a little caught up in the crazy."

He moved to stand side by side with her, but he kept his eyes on the road ahead.

"I hear they mix the drinks pretty strong."

Leslie snorted. Could be. Although she felt okay now. A little buzzed, yes, but certainly not so drunk she could blame her brazen actions on the liquor.

"That why you've been carrying a beer bottle around all night?" She flashed a grin at him, but now that he was standing so close to her, she was embarrassed to talk to him. Who had he seen her kiss? What was he thinking?

"Partly," he answered with a sheepish smile.

"Only partly?" She turned sideways to look at him.

"I'd rather just drink beer." His answer was simple. "You come here often?"

"Nope."

He nodded as if he was satisfied with her answer.

"I should…" She blinked. "Do you know the rules here tonight?" She gave him a quick once over, looking for a passport. When she lifted her gaze to meet his, his lips tilted up in a slow smile, the arch of his eyebrows suggestive. Leslie blushed and laughed out loud.

"Sort of. But I'm not a registered passport carrier."

"I wasn't aware you could opt out." She shrugged, pretty sure she'd have opted out and been a casual observer if she'd known that was a possibility. She hated to do it, but she needed to check on Whitney. "I need to check on my friend."

He nodded.

"But?" He tucked his chin and gave her a curious look.

"Did you get a poker chip?"

"Nope."

She pulled hers from her pocket and held it out to him. "I'm supposed to find someone to kiss goodnight. And when I do, I'm supposed to give him a poker chip. And the person with the most poker chips at the end of the night gets a special prize."

The guy took a drink of his beer and studied her carefully.

"What if I don't see you again before I leave?"

"I probably can't win anyway. I'm not playing."

She was glad for the cover of darkness, because discussing the fact that she wanted to kiss him goodnight made her blush. "I don't care."

He laughed. "Well, then maybe you should kiss me now."

"Can I?"

"I'm not gonna stop you, if that's what you're asking."

Leslie laughed, nervous now, and moved closer to him. She stood on her tiptoes and pressed her lips to his for a quick kiss. His lips were warm, and she felt a quick thrill of electricity shoot down through her belly. She wanted to lick him, slide her tongue over his lips and taste his beer. But when she leaned back to look up at him, the heels of her sandals sunk into the wet grass, and she wobbled a bit. Embarrassed again, she decided to settle for the quick peck and go inside to check on Whitney.

"Seems a little PG for what I've been seeing at this party."

She nodded, shrugged helplessly, and stepped back.

"Yeah, kind of. But still my favorite kiss of the night."

5

"I think you can do better than that."

It might have been the almost boyish grin, the way the corner of his lips hitched up just so, or it might have been the amusement in his eyes, the way the skin around his eyes crinkled as he watched her consider his challenge. And, Leslie knew, it was still quite possible it was the liquor and the sexual charge in the air that drew her to him.

Still standing by the gate in the yard, she felt a chill on her skin and rubbed her arms vigorously.

"I can promise you she's fine." His voice dipped a little lower, and the sexy rumble strummed low in her belly and straight to the girl parts she'd neglected for far too long. "Frank and Donna run a tight ship."

Leslie wanted to laugh, but she couldn't catch her breath. The same chill that chased over her bare skin drew her nipples into tight little beads that ached so badly she wanted to rub them herself.

"Well, if I have to kiss you again to make sure you'll keep the poker chip..." She finally shrugged, but she felt a smile playing at her own lips. Sexy shoulders amped up his own grin and dragged his intense green-eyed gaze down over her body, taking excruciating care to linger at her hotspots.

"What happens if I don't accept it?"

"I guess I'll go home disappointed," she answered simply. She was glad for the cover of night, because her brazen words lit her face on fire. Shoulders lifted his hand and reached toward her. Leslie's belly flipflopped and crashed into the shot of desire raging upward from her girl parts to her heart. Shoulders only took her martini from her, but when he turned to put her drink and his beer bottle down near the fence—careful that neither tipped over—her hands shook so badly, she shook them out and then dragged her palms over the seat of her jeans.

The grin was gone when he straightened and turned back to her. Leslie caught her breath again when he stepped closer to her; his face now a mask of desire. Not that she'd ever seen the look on any other man's face. Except in the movies, maybe. She didn't have time to marvel at the thought, though, because Shoulders cupped her face in his hands and smoothed his thumbs over her lips.

It crossed her mind that she was supposed to be kissing him, but it felt right to let him take control. She moved without thought and felt her middle pressed hard to his, his arousal unmistakable. Head tipped back, she watched him drink her in, ready when he finally bent his head to kiss her.

Unlike the party kisses earlier, this felt both bold and fragile. He moved his lips over hers cautiously, his hands sliding back to cup her cheeks and his fingers playing in her hair. Leslie shivered at the touch of his skin on the back of her neck. From the far side of the yard, she heard the electronic beat of dance music and laughter and catcalls from the pool games. But none of it mattered now.

The kisses still slow, his lips still closed over hers, Leslie's heart raced. She lifted her hands to his arms, moaning with appreciation when her fingers molded his biceps. Her whole body—her toes, even—vibrated with sexual need and energy, and she whimpered with relief when he parted his lips and his warm breath feathered over her mouth. The taste of beer hit her tongue, and she opened her mouth, hungry for him. When he still teased, his lips there and gone and there again over hers, she smoothed her hands up over his shoulders and nipped at him. Her nipples throbbed painfully, and heat pooled between her thighs when she caught the tip of his tongue in her teeth.

As if she'd flipped a switch inside him, he moved everywhere at once. One hand cupped the back of her head to hold her still as his mouth plundered hers. The other slid down her back and cupped her ass cheek. Leslie lifted her leg and wrapped her thigh around his waist as he lifted her easily. Caught up in the feel of his hot, velvety tongue on hers, she wound her arms around his neck. He turned with her still in his arms and took a few steps closer to the garage. The top part of the wall was covered in vinyl-siding, but Leslie wouldn't have noticed if he'd rested her against brick. The hand on her ass stroked over her thigh and her knee and back to her ass, his tongue dancing with hers. She met him stroke for stroke and grinded her hips into his center when he cupped her ass in that hand again. Desperate for pressure, for friction between her legs, she moaned softly in protest when he broke the kiss and backed away from her.

"I still don't think I'm ready to take the poker chip." His voice was gruff, his chest huffing as he chased his breath. Leslie rested her head on the wall and nibbled on her lip as she watched him watch her. He played with her hair for a moment and then those same fingers slid over her lips and down over her chin to her neck.

"Are you gonna send me home like this?"

"I don't wanna send you home disappointed." Eyes locked

with hers, he shook his head slightly as his fingers worked the buttons on her blouse. Leslie's heartbeat pounded in her throat, louder and faster than the ever-present beat of the party music. Blouse unbuttoned, Shoulders parted it with his fingers and then explored the soft skin of her smooth belly.

She wished she were naked, but the thought of stopping him so she could sit up and shrug out of the blouse irritated her. She wanted his mouth on her skin, his fingers on her breasts. As if he could read her mind, he pushed the cups of her bra up and feasted his eyes on her bare breasts. Her nipples were long and hard, begging for his touch.

He thumbed one and then the other, his eyes on hers as he did so. Leslie hissed and bucked against him, a thrill shooting through her veins when she felt the press of his erection against her center.

"More. Please."

He moved his other hand—her back still propped against the wall—to touch her. Leslie squeezed her legs tighter around his waist as he played with her nipples, beading, pinching them hard enough that she cried out.

"Please."

The voice that came from her lips wasn't her own. She'd never heard herself sound so sultry, so desperate. When he only weighed the curves of her breasts in his hands, she groaned and closed her eyes. He rocked his hips against hers, the contact between her legs igniting a fire inside her.

"You're beautiful." He pressed his lips to the underside of her chin, making her wish again that she was naked. She wanted his tongue everywhere, without barriers between them. Her eyes flew open when his lips suddenly closed over her nipple and tugged deliciously hard.

"Please." She moaned again and then whispered and cried softly when he turned his attention to her other breast and dragged his teeth over her sensitive skin. "I need you. Please."

"You need to come, beautiful." He whispered the words over her damp skin. Leslie shivered when a chill chased them, and then she whimpered again when he unbuttoned her jeans. "Let me make you come."

"Yes. Please, yes." She lowered her legs to the ground, and even without the heeled sandals, she would have teetered on her trembling legs. With his attention on her zipper, his hands inching her jeans and her white lace panties down over her hips, the night air was cool on her bare breasts. Her nipples tightened again, and Leslie reached to rub them, to both ease and prolong the pleasure pain.

"That's so fucking beautiful." He slowed his hands, her ass cheeks bared, and watched her smooth her hands over her breasts. "Play for me, gorgeous."

"Touch me." She panted and rolled her nipples between her fingers and thumbs.

He eased himself down her body, flicking both nipples and her fingers with his tongue as he went. Kneeling before her, he pushed his hands inside her jeans again and molded the backs of her thighs as he pulled the denim further down her legs.

Leslie's heartbeat jumped again when he reached to touch her panties and then lifted his eyes to hers.

"Your panties are soaked, sweetheart."

In the shadows, she thought she saw his lips twitch up in a smile, but she couldn't be sure.

"If you give me that poker chip, I want your panties, too."

"You want my panties?" Her mouth was dry, but no wonder, as every drop of moisture in her body was between her legs.

"I do."

"Okay."

"Play," he reminded her.

She did as he asked, the need, the heat reaching boiling

point as he watched her tweak and pinch her nipples. Her knees buckled when he touched her. Just the press of his fingertips on her thighs. The drag of his fingertips over the backs of her knees. The pressure of his hands cupping her bare ass.

"Please?" she said again.

"Please what?"

"Please touch me."

"I am touching you, angel, and I love how soft your skin is."

She mewled in protest when he continued the slow, gentle strokes, the torturous glide of his fingers over the backs of her knees.

"What do you want me to touch?"

"Make me come." The words were both desperate and commanding, and suddenly, his fingers tightened around her thighs and he spread her open with his thumbs. He licked her seam and then blew gently over her clit as he lifted his eyes to hers again.

"I love the way you taste," he told her. Leslie opened her mouth to urge him to do it again, but he moved before she could speak. He spread her open wider, and then as he brushed kisses over her dark curls, he eased his fingers inside her and pressed his thumb over her clit.

"Oh, God," she moaned her appreciation and rested her head on the wall at her back. Eyes closed, she heard the music in the background and felt the beat in her chest. Hands still playing with her breasts, she tried to open her legs further to give him better access to her sensitive parts.

"I've got you, beautiful," he promised. "You just relax and let me take care of you."

He stroked her with slow, intense movements. His thumbs pinched and pressed over her clit as he scissored his fingers deep inside her. His hot breath on her skin was at odds with the cool night air around them. Leslie dropped one hand to his head and dragged her fingers through his hair. His open mouth pressed to her clit, she heard him moan when she tugged the ponytail holder from his hair.

Her stranger with the sexy, wide shoulders sucked her clit into his mouth and flicked it with his tongue and then came up for air, driving her to the edge and then yanking her back, over and over, until she felt the heat—the explosion ready to tear her apart—and then she held his head, pressed him close and chanted yes, yes, yes. He gave in and curled his fingers inside her as he licked her clit with the perfect pressure.

"OH." She tensed as she came, shouting an oh god—she didn't even know his name—and her fingers went lax in his hair. He didn't stop, didn't let up. His fingers still rubbed the perfect spot and rhythm inside her, and though he added a thumb to the play at her clit, he continued to lick and lap between her legs. Her knees buckled when she came again, and this time, her sexy stranger smoothed his hands up the back of her thighs and cupped her ass again as he slowly stood.

"That was the sexiest thing I've seen all night," he told her. "And maybe all year."

Still panting with her release, Leslie lifted her head to kiss him, turned on again when she tasted herself on his lips and his tongue. His kiss was gentle now; his hands caressing her softly.

"Maybe ever," he decided.

She stared at him silently when he drew back from her.

"Are you okay?"

She nodded and offered him a small smile. "I'm still...in the clouds. You just lit up that sky with a million stars."

"So, I'm not sending you home disappointed?" He cocked his head and arched his eyebrows as he tugged her bra back down to cover her breasts.

"God, no."

"Good."

His grin was all cocky-male. Leslie pushed her hips into his as he slowly buttoned her blouse again. She wanted more. She wanted to redo all of it. She wanted to rip his clothes off and run her tongue over him, starting with his shoulders and down over his cock and to his feet.

"What about you?"

"Trust me, sweetheart." He kissed her again, but it was just a soft, sweet touch of his lips over hers. "I'm gonna take your panties home with me, and I'm gonna sleep with them, and I'm gonna dream about my face in your pussy."

Leslie wobbled on Whitney's heels.

Dammit. For the first time in her life, she wanted to leave a party with a total stranger. She wanted to get naked and open her mouth, her legs, for this delicious man, and she couldn't. She had come here with Whitney, and though her friend was okay inside with other friends, she did need to get back to her and check on her.

"And then what?"

Her bold whisper shocked her, and she almost opened her mouth to gobble the words back up. Her sexy stranger knelt in front of her again. Leslie watched him as he lifted her foot and slipped the sandal off. Her heart punched wildly in her chest when she realized he was really going to take her panties.

Together they worked the lace off and her jeans back on and up over her hips without Leslie's bare feet touching the wet grass. It occurred to her that his jeans would be wet in the knees, and she wondered if he would go back inside like that or if he would leave.

"I'm pretty fucking glad I didn't have a passport," he announced as he dipped his head to kiss her again.

"I am, too." She nodded and stared up at him with a head

full of worries and a heart full of wishes. She wanted more, and though she was still floating over the two orgasms he'd just given her, she felt a little stab of worry or regret that she hadn't done anything for him. "Are you going home disappointed?"

"Sweetheart, that was so incredible. I had the best time of anyone at this party."

"Except for me," she said with a little giggle.

"I sure hope so."

He kissed her again. Reluctant to let the night be over, Leslie held him tight.

"If you rock those hips against me one more time, I'm gonna come in my jeans." His tone held a warning. "I don't kiss and tell, sweetheart. But I don't wanna walk back in the house and have them think I was out here jacking off all alone."

"They won't." She shook her head. "The knees of your jeans are wet."

6

They stayed until midnight. Leslie checked on Whitney and found her playing *Dirty Word Scrabble*. At Whitney's insistence, she joined the game and played for a while, but her brain and her body—especially her body—was still outside, plastered up against the wall with a stranger's mouth between her legs.

She moved to the *Dirty Pictures* table when Whitney did, still in enough of a fog that she didn't pause to wonder if Whitney had wondered where she'd gone. She refused to play strip poker but joined some made up game of *If I could, I would...*that made Leslie think of a weird version of *Never Have I Ever* or *Truth or Dare*. Luckily, she'd dodged the bullet in that one. She wasn't sure what she'd fill in the blank with anyway. *If I could, I would chase after Shoulders and put my hands and mouth all over him* felt a bit too revealing for her, even if what she'd done with the stranger was all new ground for her.

When she and Whitney left, the party was still going, and Frank insisted they take a breathalyzer test on the way out. Leslie could have told him they were both fine; she knew

Whitney well enough to know that. Leslie had switched to water after the second martini, and Whitney had a couple bottles of water and then a beer.

"Here." Whitney handed her the keys to the Jetta as they crossed the street.

"Really?" Leslie looked at her with concern.

"Well, technically, I drank more than you." She shrugged. "I feel fine, but maybe it's better."

"Okay."

They climbed into the Jetta. Buckled up. Leslie checked over her shoulder before she pulled away from the curb.

"That was the most bizarre party I've ever been to."

Bizarre, but after what she'd done outside with the sexy stranger, she wouldn't say she didn't have fun. She wasn't sure what to say about it, so for the time being, she kept her mouth shut. Part of her was dying to tell Whitney—after all, they'd always been pretty open, except maybe for the sex tape Whitney and Shawn made—but she wasn't ready yet. First of all, she wanted to go home and crawl into bed and relive everything again and again. And maybe again. Maybe she would eventually tell Whitney, but sharing it this soon might take the heat out of the night and Leslie wasn't ready to do that. And oddly enough, even though the guy was a total stranger, something about what they'd shared felt special. He hadn't shoved her jeans down and banged her against the wall with a thank you or kiss my ass. He'd gone down on his knees in the wet grass and pleasured her, driving her past the first orgasm and drawing out another one before buttoning her up and kissing her goodbye.

"Tell me," Whitney mumbled.

And taking her panties. Leslie almost laughed out loud. Almost told Whitney that while her white lace bra might have been too matronly pushed up over her naked breasts, the stranger hadn't had any problems with her white lace panties as he'd shoved them in his pocket after driving her out of her mind.

He'd made a point of rubbing his thumb back and forth over the crotch of the panties—gaze locked with hers—before putting them in his pocket. He'd kissed her again. Her nipples had damned near poked a hole through the lace when they parted company. Leslie turned her head away to look out the window when she felt the grin on her face. Didn't seem like he minded the bra, either, she decided, still not looking at Whitney.

"You work with those people?"

Whitney laughed. "Well, you'd think it would make Monday mornings interesting. But if they do this sort of thing on a regular basis, I had no idea. So apparently, they're all very discreet."

"Do any of them have kids?"

"Yeah. Donna and Frank have two daughters and a son. I know several of them have kids. They're dance moms and honor student parents and football parents. Dads who coach. Members of the PTA."

"Hmm." Leslie shook her head. "Well, I had planned to go home and read. I think this might have been more entertaining, but I'm not sure I could ever do that again."

Well. She could happily meet up with the stranger with the talented tongue and hands again. The party, she could take or leave, no big deal.

When she had gone inside, the stranger had gone to the bar. Despite telling herself not to look back, of course she'd done it. Looked back at him over her shoulder. Longneck bottle in hand, he'd tipped his head at her and lifted the bottle to his mouth and licked the rim. Leslie had felt that lick as if he'd swiped his tongue over all of her still overly sensitive parts, and she'd slipped inside on wobbly knees.

Why hadn't she gotten his name?

It wasn't that kind of party, Leslie, she reminded herself. For all she knew, the guy could be married. The thought ripped through her with the force of a freight train.

When Whitney still didn't say anything, Leslie glanced at her. "What's wrong?" She held her breath, worried now that she was wearing her emotions, her memories on her sleeve.

"Nothing."

"Whit."

"I'm just tired."

Leslie drove in silence for a few minutes. She considered turning on the radio, but they were within five minutes of Whitney's place, so it seemed pointless. Worried, too, that something was bothering Whitney, she eyed her carefully a couple of times and then gave up to pull the car into the garage. Whitney was out of the car before Leslie could hit the button to shut the door.

"You wanna just stay here?" Whitney asked around a yawn as Leslie followed her through the back door. She didn't, not really. She wanted to be alone. In her own bed. To relive, recapture the way the stranger made her feel. It would be weird to do that at her friend's house. But, one look at Whitney's sad face had her nodding.

"Yeah, if you don't care."

"Nope." Whitney led her around the corner to the kitchen. Flipped on the can lights over the counter.

"What happened?" Leslie asked quietly.

"What?" Whitney, hand on the refrigerator door handle, looked at her over her shoulder.

"Did something happen when I went outside?"

"No." Whitney shook her head slowly. "Why?"

"You're acting funny. What's going on?"

Whitney sighed. She pulled the door open and grabbed a couple of water bottles. Leslie took the one she handed her and twisted the top off.

"I thought Shawn might text."

Leslie winced.

"Instead, I made the mistake of looking at his Facebook page."

"Oh, no." Leslie took a drink of her water and perched on the edge of a stool. Leaned her elbows on the deep blue granite countertop.

"Wasn't that bad," Whitney admitted. "Just posted a picture of him and the guys at the ballgame."

"And?"

"There were a couple of cute girls with them."

Leslie chewed on her lip for a second and watched Whitney pretend like it didn't really bother her.

"Maybe they're with the other guys," she suggested.

"I know." Whitney nodded. "I do. I just…hate that we had that fight. And that he's so far away right now."

"I'm sorry, Whit."

Whitney nodded again. "Where'd you go?"

Leslie watched her climb up on a barstool, leaving an empty one between them.

"Hmm?"

"When you went out for some air."

"Oh." Leslie pursed her lips. She turned her head away to hide her face from Whitney until she had her emotions—wistful, searching, and a side of guilt—under control. "Just went out and walked around the yard."

"Anyone in the pool?"

"Yep, I went the other way."

Whitney laughed and took a big drink of her water. Leslie took a deep breath and spoke, praying she sounded noncha-lant and not keyed up damned near enough to be miserable. "Did you see that guy there? With the ponytail? Sexy shoulders?"

"Huh-uh."

"Seriously? Smoldering green eyes? You missed him?"

"Apparently, I did."

"Damn." Leslie groaned. "I saw him just before we sat down to play *Spin the Bottle*."

"Did you talk to him?"

"I gave him my poker chip," Leslie hedged. She would feel bad if she flat out lied to Whitney, but somehow a lie of omission felt a little less deceitful.

"You kissed him goodnight?"

"Mm-hmm." She nodded quickly.

Whitney laughed out loud. "Tongue?"

Leslie snorted and rolled her eyes. She felt a blush creep up her neck. "Um. Yeah." She rubbed her cheeks and hoped Whitney saw her distress as embarrassment about the game and their kiss. " Jeez, Whit, that was tougher than *Spin the Bottle* when we were kids!"

"So, who was he? What's his name?"

"No idea."

"Well, damn. A ponytail guy. With sexy shoulders."

Leslie nodded. Whitney stared at something just over Leslie's shoulder. She finally shook her head. "I don't think I know him. He's not at the bank."

"Oh, well. He was fun to look at." Leslie's attempt at light-hearted fell flat. She had hoped that she could gloss over what had happened and find out that Whitney did indeed know who he was. Her disappointment was cold and hard to swallow.

"I can ask around," Whitney offered.

"No, you can't. You're not supposed to bring a party like that up at the office."

"No, but I could ask Donna. Did you, like, see him in the pool or anything?"

"Ew…no." Leslie rolled her head on her neck. "In fact, he said he didn't have a passport. Wasn't playing."

"Hmm." Whitney frowned and shrugged. "No idea."

"I think I'd have maybe opted out of carrying a passport if I'd known that was possible."

Whitney snorted. "I dunno. Looked like you were having some fun."

Leslie cringed. She laughed out loud, ducked her head, and rubbed her forehead. "It was interesting. Between French kissing my lifelong best friend and the garlic salt guy."

"Yeah, you were the best kisser, too. I'd still pick Shawn over you, but." Whitney shrugged, and then the two of them cut loose with a loud laugh.

"Did you see that guy almost sneeze? On me?"

"Was he the one you were straddling?"

Whitney's turn to look embarrassed. She chuckled quietly and shrugged.

"Yep."

"No, I missed that part. I was looking for the guy with the ponytail. Who'd you give your poker chip to?"

Whitney wiggled around on the seat and stuck her hand in her pocket. Pulled out the poker chip.

"I didn't."

"How come?"

Whitney shrugged and sighed. "By that time, I'd seen Shawn's post...and I'd kissed my lifelong best friend, which was either terribly scarring or superbly special, and how the hell was I gonna beat either of those?"

Leslie grinned.

"He'll call you."

Whitney put the poker chip down on the counter, pushed it with her index finger toward Leslie, and stood up.

"Thanks," she said quietly. "For going with me."

Leslie shrugged and nodded, offered Whitney a tired smile.

"I'm going to bed." Whitney kissed Leslie's cheek and headed back around the corner and out of the kitchen.

"Whit?" Leslie called as she slid off the barstool. She twisted the cap off her bottle, took another drink, and turned the kitchen light off.

"What?" Whitney's answer was faint, coming from the master bath.

Leslie hitched a shoulder up against the wall.

"Doesn't matter how superbly scarring it was," she said as Whitney stuck her head out her bedroom door. "Second hottest kiss I had all night, and you still owe me. Like, at least twenty. Somethings."

Whitney snorted. She cocked her head and shot Leslie a lazy grin.

"Kick me when I'm down," she said with a nod.

"Yeah, well, any luck someone else will be around to kiss it and make it better."

7

The rest of the weekend was calm by comparison. Leslie had been honest with Whitney; she wasn't particularly scarred over their kiss. But she wasn't stuck on it, either. However, she couldn't get the guy with the sexy shoulders and talented hands out of her head. Why hadn't she talked to him longer? Asked his name, at least. No, it wasn't the kind of party where you met someone and started dating. But she'd gotten the names of the people she'd kissed while playing *Spin the Bottle*. And for Pete's sake, she'd been a hell of a lot more personal with the sexy-shouldered stranger.

She'd relived the whole scene. Not the night of the shower, when she stayed at Whitney's. But from the second she'd walked into her own place Saturday morning until she'd finally gone to sleep last night, she'd remembered and relived every second of her time spent outside with the stranger.

Her emotions were at war inside. Her body desperately wanted to feel it all again. Her heart and her brain weren't sure what to think. Part of her felt guilty for not checking on Whitney sooner, for trusting the stranger when he'd said she would be fine. After all, what had he done after talking her into staying outside with him but get in her pants? Except what did he get out of that? Sure, Leslie thought he'd enjoyed it, and he'd taken her poker chip, and her panties, and her moans of pleasure, but he hadn't used her for his own pleasure. And as outrageous as the party seemed to her and Whitney, no one had been out of hand or drunk and disorderly. Neither Frank nor Donna were drinking, and they had both wandered through the party guests and games continuously to make sure things were under control. Whitney had been fine inside the house the whole time Leslie's mind and control were spinning out of her grasp.

As crazy as the whole thing was to Leslie, she had to admit that most of the party guests there behaved as if they had seen and done it all before. Even her stranger—though he didn't have a passport—didn't appear to be shocked by what he was seeing. In fact, he'd told her Frank and Donna had everything under control.

Then again, maybe he wouldn't have been comfortable with giving her his name. He had opted out of the games, so maybe he *was* married or seeing someone or just...not into adult games. Adult activities, obviously, but maybe he preferred random hook ups like theirs.

The party, the games—those were crazy, new experiences for her. But that leap of desire when she saw him in the kitchen? A mix of familiar and new and exciting. She'd felt the draw to him, a magnetic pull, in her blood, and that had been frightening. The quick kiss goodbye she'd tried to give him had been a big deal for her, but the things she'd done with him? Let him do to her? She'd never felt that kind of sexual pleasure before, which had to indicate some level of trust.

The idea of trusting a complete stranger to go down on her boggled her mind. The worry that the guy had gone home to a wife or collected a wife or girlfriend on the way out of the party made her sick with guilt and unease. The worry over what Whitney would say if she ever told her scared the hell out of her.

And still, all she could think about was the guy, the encounter, the weekend. Even with all of the misgivings, she wished she knew who he was, wished she would see him again.

The bell above the door dinged and snapped Leslie out of her thoughts. Her cheeks felt a bit warm as she looked at the middle-aged man who approached her at the counter. Hoping he didn't notice, she plastered on a big, fake smile and rested her hands on the white Formica counter.

"How can I help you?"

She almost sighed with relief when her voice sounded normal. But that might have given away her discomfort, and while this customer wouldn't ask, if Jace or any of his brothers wandered in, they sure as hell would.

"Need to pick up my rider," the guy told her.

"Great. What's the name?"

She tapped the customer's name into the computer, noted that the repair work had been completed, and picked up the cordless handset to let the guys in the shop know the customer was here.

Leslie rang the repair bill up with steady hands and made small talk with the customer, all the while thoughts of the other night vying for her attention. She had talked to Whitney yesterday, but not about THE GUY. Shawn, thank God, had called. Leslie wasn't sure her friend knew what she wanted—well, Whitney wanted the whole kit and caboodle, but slick-talking Shawn was good at putting her off. They had been together for years, on more than off, though there was no question, Shawn viewed marriage as confining and not necessarily happy. The last time they had talked about it

—a bunch of friends at a mutual friend's wedding reception —Shawn had nearly clawed his shirt collar and tie away from his neck, as if the idea of marriage strangled him.

Jace ducked his head in through the shop door and hollered to let her know that he had Mr. Magee's rider ready to load and to send the man on back. Leslie nodded, the flaming heat in her cheeks dialed uncomfortably high again. Wasn't like anybody knew what she'd done outside in the dark. The stranger wasn't going to tell anyone, and even if he did, she hadn't given him her name, either. She hadn't played any naked games. She'd caught a few eyefuls of strip poker, some accidental and some...not so much...but she hadn't dawdled around the pool at all.

Maybe it was just the idea of being at a party like that that had her blushing like a school girl. Of Jace or his brothers asking questions about it. Damn straight, they would all have loved it. Come to think of it, Leslie wondered if Whitney intended to tell Shawn about the party. Technically, they weren't supposed to discuss it with anyone, and for good reason. But on the other hand, Shawn and Whitney were a couple. Surely, that was different.

Leslie huffed out a breath of relief when Mr. Magee disappeared into the shop. The clatter of tools and the roar of a mower engine drifted into the storefront, but the room fell silent again when the door slowly swished shut. Maybe that was the problem. Maybe it was too quiet. Leslie cast a quick glance at the clock on the wall as she moved to sit at her desk.

Half an hour until lunchtime. Mondays were usually insanely busy, but today had sort of dragged. She lowered herself into her chair and perched on her bent leg.

Music. She reached for her purse, hidden in the bottom desk drawer. Pulled her phone out and noticed a text from an unknown number just as she tapped her music app.

Okay, music first, and then she would check the text, and then get busy. It was that time of the month—accounts receivable could sometimes be as bad as the girl stuff—and if she had any plans to get the bills mailed on time, she should get started on that now.

She chose Arcade Fire from her list of artists and then backed out of the app to look at the text.

Why do I feel like a winner when I only have one *poker chip?*

Leslie tried to swallow, but her mouth was dry. Heart pounding in her throat and her ears, she dropped the phone from her shaking hands and cut loose with a wild, anxious squeal. Remembering that she was at work—and worse, that she worked with a bunch of nice-looking, easy-going males —she looked up quickly, her face on fire. Thankfully, she was still alone.

How had he found her?

It had to be him, right? She hadn't really talked much to anyone other than Whitney and the guy with the shoulders. Not that she'd said that much to him. Still. Leslie propped her elbows on her desk and buried her flaming cheeks in her hands. Her skin felt feverish, which only made her blush harder.

Whitney? Had Whitney found *him*?

But wouldn't she have…told her? Warned her? Did she need a warning?

Her phone dinged with another incoming text message. She wondered when the first one had dropped in. Her pulse pounded now; her heart stuck at the base of her throat, she touched the screen of her phone and pulled the text bubble to the right to check the time-received stamp.

11:19.

Eleven minutes ago.

Leslie?

With cold, clammy fingers, she picked up the phone and reminded herself to breathe.

"Les?"

Just about to answer, her thumb on the screen, she jerked to attention when she heard Jace call her name.

"Hmm?"

He moseyed a few steps into the room, and Leslie's music was drowned out by the sounds from the shop. She dropped her phone like a kid caught with her hand in the cookie jar and stood up, cursing her flaming cheeks again.

"Do you need something?" Her voice was an octave too high, and Jace knew her well enough to know she was hiding something. He probably thought she was looking at porn on her phone. Another flash of heat surged up her neck and into her face.

Why was she behaving like this? So, some guy had texted her, for Pete's sake. A guy who had performed oral sex on her and driven her past the first orgasm—she'd never come twice like that, so close together, with a guy licking her that way. Just because someone texted her didn't mean Jace was going to see through her and know what she'd done the other night.

And even if he did, so what? She hadn't done anything wrong.

"No." Jace, hands on his hips now, shook his head. He studied her with an intensity that made her want to squirm, but she forced herself to stand still and meet his gaze boldly. "Just wanted to tell you we're going to lunch."

"Oh." Her body almost buckled in relief. She nodded, leaned forward to rest her hands on her desk, and offered Jace a smile. At least she hoped it was a smile, and that she wasn't wearing some sort of plastic, scary grimace.

"Want anything?"

She opened her mouth to answer him, but her brain

flashed her a picture of the sexy stranger—the one who was apparently texting her! She needed to answer him!—and she couldn't find her voice.

"We're going to Bub's Subs." Jace lifted a hand and absently rubbed his head. Leslie noticed sweat and dirt streaked over his face. She had to bite her lip to keep from laughing out loud. He thought it was hot out there?

"No, thanks." The words slipped out before she realized she was going to speak. But she didn't want anything. Other than for him to get out of the store, so she could look at her phone again.

"Okay." He nodded. "Back in an hour."

"'kay." She stood watch as he backed toward the door. Kept the smile firmly in place and nodded at him again when he finally turned and yanked the door open. When he was gone, she dropped into her seat again and picked up her phone.

He hadn't texted again, but then, could she blame him? He was cold-texting her after a surreal party and a random hook up. He had no idea how she would respond.

She stared at the phone for a few seconds, heart rate jacked up to miserably scared out of her wits again. Took a deep breath and touched the screen with her thumb, so she could text Shoulders back.

Yes.

Done. Okay. She breathed deeply, nodded to herself, and put her phone down again. Eyed the screen. Waited for those three quivering dots to tell her he was answering her. Wondered if she'd blown her shot at getting to know him when he didn't answer her within five seconds.

"You're being ridiculous," she told herself as she deliberately spun her chair to the left and turned her back to the phone. She had work to do. The guy had probably moved on by now, anyway.

She settled her hands over her keyboard. Gave herself a mental shake and then reached for the mouse. Clicked on the shortcut to the office accounts receivable program and jumped out of her chair when her phone dinged again. She wanted to dive for it, but she made herself turn slowly and reach for it.

Whitney.

Disappointed, she read the text from her friend.

Shawn wants to do dinner tonight.

Isn't that good? Leslie typed with a frown.

No. It's Monday. It's his golf night.

Leslie winced. Okay, maybe that wasn't good, but she couldn't agree with Whitney. Best friend duty and all. It was her job to build Whitney up, at least until something seriously bad happened, and then her job would change to telling Whitney she could find someone so much better than Shawn.

Maybe he misses you.

Maybe he needs to confess that he slept with one of those girls.

Are you going to tell him about—

Leslie's heart skipped when a text dropped in from the unknown number. Feeling like the worst sort of scum, she jumped to that thread and left Whitney hanging.

Asher. Asher Collins.

Knowing she was alone, she threw her head back to rest on her chair and reveled in the warmth that flowed through her body. *Asher.*

The guy had a name. A sexy, mysterious name.

Hi Asher.

She chewed on her lip, thumb hovering over the send button. Was she supposed to say something flirty? Sexy? How the hell did she know? Yes, she had dated, and she wasn't a virgin to many experiences out there, but she

certainly wasn't an expert on men or orgasms after oral sex
with random men, either.

Les? Do you think he did?—Whitney. Damn. She forgot
about Whitney. *I mean, you aren't saying anything. You aren't
defending him, like you think he—*

Hi.

Oh, for fuck's sake. The heat in her cheeks shot straight
down, like an arrow, to all the girl stuff. And all he said
was hi.

*Whit? I don't believe Shawn did anything that would hurt you.
Can you give me a minute?*

She switched back to the other thread and stared at the
exchanges.

Sure. You okay?—Whitney.

She read that one as it dropped, but she didn't bother to
switch back. Instead, she watched the thread with Asher and
waited for the floating dots to appear. When none did, she
groaned out loud. Restless, she reached over her desk and
grabbed a pen to scribble on the desk calendar. She couldn't
draw a head on a stick figure, so instead, she colored patterns
in the numbers on the days.

Three minutes later, when there were still no floating
dots indicating that he was texting her back, she rolled her
chair back and climbed to her feet. Stalked around the storefront, one hand wrapped around the phone like it was the
hilt of a knife and she was in a dark, scary alley, and the other
straightening mower parts and lawn care items on the
shelves as she passed.

She jumped when the phone vibrated in her hand. The
default ringtone played through the storefront, but she still
stood and gaped at the phone in her hand like she wasn't sure
what to do with it.

That number was calling her.

Asher was calling her.

She smoothed her hand over the butt of her jeans and lifted the other to her ear.

"Hello?"

"Leslie?" His voice was low and sexy in her ear.

Another stab of heat shot down through her belly to her girl parts. Her thighs quivered so badly, she had to slink back to her desk and fall into her chair.

"Hi."

"I hope it's okay that I got your number."

Okay? That he got her number? Was he kidding?

She nodded and then realized he couldn't see her, so she tried to sneak a deep breath for courage and then prayed that she sounded normal when she spoke again.

"Yeah, it's…it's fine."

"Great. Are you working?"

She had been hunched over near her desk—trying to hold herself together—but at his question, she straightened and looked around frantically. Was he outside? Did he know where she worked?

"Yes, I am."

"Where do you work?"

"Hardin Landscaping," she answered automatically, thankful that at least she hadn't said it in that happy camper tone she used with customers on the business phone.

"Okay. I won't keep you. I just wanted to see if you might be free for dinner tonight."

Dinner. Tonight.

Dinner? Tonight?

She wondered if he could hear her heart pounding out her ear and over the phone line.

"Um. Yeah. I'm free. I could…do dinner."

"Great. I'll pick you up at seven."

The call went dead before she could ask him how he would know where to pick her up. She struggled to calm herself, just in case a customer came in or in case the guys had decided to grab subs and bring them back here to eat. The fire in her face raged on, though, and she breathed like she had just run wind sprints.

Les? Hello? You okay?—Whitney again.

Rather than text her friend, Leslie tapped her name on her favorites list to call her. She paced the storefront while she waited for Whitney to pick up.

8

Leslie was knee-deep in skinnies and short skirts and blouses when her doorbell rang. Standing in her bedroom, wearing nothing but a triangular scrap of pale blue lace between her legs and two small triangles of the same material over her small, round breasts, she gasped in panic and looked at the clock.

6:17.

Okay. It wasn't Asher, but she was quickly running out of time trying to decide what to wear for dinner. Less than an hour before he would be here to pick her up.

Which meant her visitor had to be Whitney. She had told her earlier that Asher had texted and then called her to ask her to dinner. What she hadn't told her was anything else, including the fact that Asher had gone home with her panties in his pocket last Saturday night. Whitney had sworn she hadn't done any digging to find out who the guy was or put a bug in his ear that Leslie was interested.

Relief flooded through her, leaving her feeling like a wet noodle. Whitney would know just what she should wear; Whitney would dress her like a doll.

Leslie stepped over a small pile of clothing—two pairs of jeans, a black dress, and a white blouse—to make her way out of her room and to the door. Remembering that she wasn't dressed, she stopped and picked her way back through the clothing options scattered on the floor to grab her robe.

Just in case it wasn't Whitney at the door. Good grief, she didn't want to traumatize anyone. Or embarrass herself.

She tied the pink sash around her waist as the doorbell rang again.

"I'm coming, I'm coming," she mumbled as she rushed out of her bedroom again and through the living room to the front door. Whitney stood on the stoop, head bent and smooth ponytail hanging around her graceful neck. Leslie watched with amusement as her friend continued to dig through her oversized bag. "What are you doing?" she finally asked when a minute had passed, and Whitney still hadn't come up for air.

Whitney held her finger up to ask for a second and then she laughed and let her bag fall to hang from her shoulder and met Leslie's gaze.

"I was looking for my key so I could get in," she said with a grin. "Clearly, you're having a fashion emergency. You need me."

It hit Leslie suddenly that Whitney was supposed to have had a date tonight.

"Wait." She shook her head. Whitney let her eyes travel from Leslie's head down to her toes and then back up to meet Leslie's gaze again. She made a show of looking at her watch and then looked back at Leslie.

"Are you wearing that?"

"No." Leslie groaned.

"Then let me in." Whitney rolled her eyes as she stepped inside, forcing Leslie to take a step back.

"I thought you were supposed to see Shawn tonight." Leslie frowned as Whitney closed the door.

"I did." Whitney nodded. She grabbed Leslie's wrist and dragged her back to her bedroom.

"For dinner."

"Well, we had a quick dinner," Whitney explained. "He has golf—"

"League." Leslie nodded. "Yeah, I know. But—? You already had dinner?"

Whitney grinned as she slung her purse down on Leslie's made bed, which was also covered in odd clothing items.

"Good grief, woman." Whitney sighed and pinched the bridge of her nose, as if she didn't know where to begin and was overwhelmed. "We had dinner. He said he missed me. That he hated being in Texas, and he's coming over later."

"And?"

"And what?" Whitney turned her back to Leslie and fixed her attention on the closet. "Is there anything left in there?"

"Did you talk about the fact that you broke up? Are you getting back together? And yes, there's still stuff in the closet. As you can see."

"Well, yeah, we're together." Whitney propped her hands on her hips and surveyed the contents of Leslie's closet. "Why are freaking out about this date?"

"Um." Leslie blinked and threw her hands up defensively. "Because I have no idea where we're going. Because I don't know him. Never talked to him before that night. In the dark outside of a sex party. Where he was—"

"It wasn't a sex party," Whitney corrected her. "It was a wedding shower. With sex games."

"How's that different from a sex party?" Leslie tipped her head when Whitney looked at her over her shoulder.

"I don't know." Whitney shook her head. "It's more than that."

"What do you mean?"

"You are like...so hung up...on this guy."

"You didn't see him," Leslie reminded her friend, but she ducked her head to avoid direct eye contact. She should have told Whitney what happened. They were best friends, and they shared things. They often overshared things.

Now wasn't the right time, though. Not with the fashion emergency and the fact that Asher would be there to get her in less than an hour.

"I've never seen you go nuts over a guy's looks. Like sure, we talk about hot guys, but this is different."

The suspicious look on Whitney's face and the interrogation-like questions made Leslie squirm on the bed. She felt her mouth working, as if she was actually going to try to explain the way her body had nearly combusted when her eyes met his—it felt weird to think of him as Asher, since she hadn't officially met him yet. Whitney watched her, eyes wide with interest.

"I don't know, Whit," she finally mumbled. "There was just something...about him." Tomorrow. Tomorrow, she would meet Whitney after work, they could grab a drink, and she would tell all. Surely Whitney would forgive her for holding out on her, wouldn't she?

"Apparently." Whitney pursed her lips. "So, what's the goal here?"

"What?" Leslie looked desperately at the clock on her nightstand when Whitney sat down beside her on the edge of the bed.

"Get to know him. See him again? Another kiss goodnight?" Whitney shrugged. "Or more?"

"I don't know."

The words were out of her mouth before she realized she was going to answer. What was she going to say? Did she want a nice dinner and a kiss goodnight? Well....didn't she want that? Isn't that what she always expected from a date? A good time that led to the possibility of a second and maybe third date?

Or did she want more?

She wanted more. She wanted a repeat of last Saturday's oral sex and the orgasms, and she wanted to put her mouth on him. She'd dreamt about that, about taking him in her mouth and making his heart race like he'd done to her. She wanted him on top of her, his weight pressing her to the mattress and that massive erection inside her. But she wasn't prepared to say that to Whitney. Not at the moment.

She wanted some fun dialogue, too. She wanted to get to know him. A phone call tomorrow. Another date soon.

"Did you shave your legs?" Whitney's eyes grew wide with surprise when Leslie blushed.

"Yes."

"You're gonna have sex with him?" Whitney's laugh was soft and sultry, but when the pink in Leslie's cheeks grew hotter, she let out a whoop and jumped off the bed. "You're gonna have sex with him."

"I don't know!" Leslie lunged for her friend and caught her wrists in her hands. "Whit, I have no idea what's going to happen."

"But you're thinking about it." Whitney tilted her head and narrowed her eyes at Leslie.

"Maybe." Leslie shrugged one shoulder and then cringed, waiting for Whitney's response.

"Okay." Whitney nodded. "Let's see it."

"What?"

"Drop the robe." Whitney rolled her eyes. "For Pete's sake, my tongue was in your mouth last weekend. What are you wearing?"

Leslie laughed and drew in a deep breath to summon her courage. Not just for this moment; after all, they'd been friends for years and had dressed for nights out together before. Just not quite like this. With Whitney as the fashion guru, scrutinizing Leslie's underwear choices, with the thought of Leslie having sex with Asher lingering between them.

At the moment, she needed courage for what happened the second Whitney left her house and Asher arrived.

Whitney tugged one hand loose of Leslie's grasp and reached to yank the sash of her robe open.

"I feel like you're manhandling me," Leslie said with a laugh.

"Woman-handling?" Whitney shrugged her lips. "Is that a thing?"

Leslie shrugged out of the robe and let it fall to the floor.

"Ha. Damn. That was sexy." Whitney nodded her approval. "And holy smokin' lingerie. You look delicious."

"Um." Leslie frowned and looked at her friend through an uncertain squint. "Thanks?"

"Yep. I'd totally do you, if...you know..." Whitney shook her head. "Okay. First date. Don't know him well. What was he wearing last weekend?"

"Jeans," Leslie answered simply, crossing her fingers behind her back that Whitney would forgive her when she finally came clean. "And a t-shirt. That sort of...molded those broad shoulders. Emphasized his chest. Kind of tight on his biceps..."

Whitney stared at her, eyebrows half way up her forehead. "Uh-huh. Anything else you need to share? Maybe about how his jeans fit him?"

Leslie cleared her throat.

"There's something you're not telling me."

"Whit." Leslie sighed and then groaned, frustrated with herself and with Whitney for picking this particular moment to zero in on Leslie's secret.

"Do you wanna look sweet and feminine? Hot and sexy? Easy access?"

Leslie looked back over her shoulder at the clock again. "Whit, in twenty minutes, he'll be here, and I'll be wearing blue lace."

Whitney swung her gaze around the room and then clicked her eyes back on Leslie's.

"Yeah, you can't have sex here. Not when every horizontal surface in here is covered with clothes."

"Not helping!"

"Okay." Whitney turned back to the closet. "Okay. Right. I think a dress."

"Really?"

"Yes. Casual. Flirty."

Leslie sighed with relief when Whitney started scooching the hangers around in the closet, actively looking for the perfect dress. Butterflies danced in her belly, and there was a familiar ache lower, between her thighs. The possibilities tonight offered tickled at the edge of her awareness, like a feather tracing up her spine. Whitney finally pulled a creme-colored sleeveless dress from a hanger and turned to Leslie.

"Really?"

"Mm-hmm." Whitney nodded. "Perfect with the tan."

Leslie didn't hate it, but she didn't love it. She did trust Whitney, though. She slipped the dress over her head and smoothed the short skirt over her hips. Whitney studied her thoughtfully and stepped closer to tug and adjust the bodice and the shoulders. She nodded and then went back to the closet in search of shoes.

Leslie prayed she didn't pull any ridiculous heels out. And then offered a silent thank you to the god of first dates when Whitney produced a pair of creme-colored wedge sandals.

"No color?" Leslie asked as she stepped into the sandals.

Whitney didn't answer her, just cupped her chin in her

hands and twisted her face this way and that. Leslie had redone her hair and makeup earlier, so she was relieved once again when Whitney nodded her approval.

"Sleek and sexy," she said as she slipped past Leslie to rummage through her jewelry box. Leslie sucked in a nervous breath as she stepped up to the closet door to check her look in the mirror there. She had to hand it to Whitney; she looked casual but confident. Summery. The dress clung to her hips and her breasts, the V-neck offering a nice slice of cleavage.

"And these."

Whitney stepped up behind her and held a big gold hoop to her ear.

"Classic."

Leslie took the earrings from her and ducked her head to first one side and then the other to put the earrings in. She wouldn't have chosen this dress for the date, but she was pleased with the outcome.

"You're on the pill?" Whitney stepped back to survey her work.

Leslie rolled her eyes. "Have been for years."

"Use a condom, though," Whitney reminded her. "Promise."

"Whitney."

"I want details."

"No."

"Yes. And I want details about whatever it is you haven't told me yet about last weekend. How many times have I shared details with you?"

"Because I'm single, and you have sex whenever you want it."

"Still." Whitney winked. "This guy blew your mind, Leslie. Like, you wandered out of a sex party to find him—"

"First." Leslie watched as Whitney started gathering her clothes up from the floor and the bed. "What're you doing?"

"Picking up. In case he brings you home for sex."

Leslie gasped out loud at the mental image of Asher, naked, in her bed. His hair fanned out on her sheets. Her comforter pulled just so, low over his hips. His cock hard and ready—

"Leslie? First?"

Leslie cleared her throat. "It wasn't a sex party. Remember?"

"Oh, the hell it wasn't." Whitney laughed out loud.

"And besides that, I didn't leave the party to go looking for him—"

Whitney threw her head back and cut loose a throaty laugh. "And the hell you didn't!"

9

W hitney left Leslie's house at 6:55. Her bedroom was spotless—unless you counted the closet, and Leslie didn't—and Leslie certainly felt more put together in the classy, crème dress and wedges than if she had tried to pull something together for this first date.

Was it a date? Would they see each other again? Was she really going to worry about it now? Leslie felt as if she'd stepped into a parallel world last weekend at that party. Mostly, things had all slid back into place. She was back at work, selling mower parts and soothing disgruntled customers, and watching Jace Hardin and thinking he was a nice guy and why couldn't things have just worked out for them?

Except that when she closed her eyes, she saw the images from the party. The passports. The *Spin the Bottle* group— guys, girls, old, young, you name it—gathered in a circle on the area rug in the living area in a house far more elegant than Leslie was used to. She could still feel the kisses—the firm, warm lips on hers and yes, that kiss with Whitney was still there, though thankfully, it hadn't proved to be an issue between them since it happened.

She had dreamt about the pool.

Finding her stranger—Asher—in the pool. Waiting for her.

Unfortunately, her alarm clock Monday morning put an end to that before it got too far. Leslie could feel the cool, silky water of the pool lapping at her thighs as she slid off the side. Asher watched with intense eyes; his shoulders bare and broad with muscles drawing her eye. She would love to go back to that dream and feel the water as it covered her belly and her breasts and smooth her hands over Asher's hard, muscular arms.

The ring of the doorbell jarred her out of those thoughts. Standing in the kitchen now, electricity pumping through her body after thinking about the dream, Leslie wrung her hands. This was it. That body, that man with the intense eyes and the delicious-looking shoulders, was on the other side of her door. She wasn't necessarily the type of woman to throw the door open, invite him in, and strip her clothes off. But she reminded herself as she finally took a step toward the door, she was a grown woman, and she was perfectly capable of making her own decisions.

If tonight was just dinner, that was okay with her.

If tonight was dinner followed by down and dirty sex—in Asher's car or up against the wall by her front door—well, that was okay, too.

That thought in mind, Leslie opened the door, ready to greet Asher and go to dinner like any other adult woman would. The air sparked with that same, smoldering tension from the party when their eyes met. Asher reveled in the power he had over her. His eyes seemed to drink her in, to beckon her to come closer. Leslie's body was enflamed; fire licked the sensitive skin of her lips and her inner wrists and her nipples.

"Hi."

Leslie's eyes were drawn to his lethal smile. She'd kissed those lips. She'd been bold enough to stand on her tiptoes and kiss this beautiful stranger goodbye last weekend. Bold enough to climb his body like a tree and wrap her limbs around him to hang on. Bold enough to stand before him and take what he gave her as those lips and his tongue and his hands worshipped her.

"Hi."

"I'm Asher." He eased up on the smolder, and the lethal smile became a sexy grin.

Leslie's legs were a little unsteady as she reached to shake the hand he offered. Suddenly shy, she ducked her chin and bit her lip.

"Leslie."

She looked at him through her lashes, from under the longer, loose blonde chunk of hair that fell over her eye and saw him step closer. His thigh brushed hers; the slide of soft denim over her bare knee under the hem of her dress made her catch her breath.

Still holding her hand in his, Asher cupped her elbow in his free hand and leaned in to press a soft kiss to her cheek.

"It's good to see you again, Leslie."

Okay, so the guy could be a real player. Maybe this was his game. Observe at Frank and Donna's parties and pick out an average Josephine and pursue her. Dazzle her. Take her to bed. Game over.

Leslie's eyelids were heavy, her body tingly and floaty as she breathed deeply and inhaled Asher's masculine scent. The cologne was understated, fresh and clean, and Leslie wanted to take a bite. His face pressed close to her, she could feel the warmth of his skin. She had the fleeting thought to taste him, to close her teeth over his earlobe and pull gently.

If he was a player, Leslie would be a finely tuned instrument, ready for his fingers to pluck and stroke and coax beautiful music from her body. She wanted more, but she decided to take whatever the night, whatever Asher offered.

"You look beautiful."

His voice was low and smooth, like whisky on the rocks. Leslie's pulse was thick and slow in her throat. She blinked and lifted her chin to look at him as he stepped back from her. His eyes—deep, forest green with flecks of gold—held hers for a beat of silence.

She shivered as he stroked his fingers back over her arm, over that sensitive skin at her wrist that was already warm. Maybe she would do well to remember that most likely Asher was a player, but on the other hand, why not enjoy the seduction? She could enjoy the sex and walk away. No reason her heart had to get involved at all.

"Rossi's okay?"

"Yes." Leslie nodded. She stepped back from him, regretting the distance between them immediately, and grabbed her small clutch purse from the arm of the sofa. She took a quick peek to make sure her keys and phone were in the purse and then stepped out on the stoop with him. Asher's big body was warm and solid behind her as she pulled the door closed and then jiggled the handle to be sure it was locked.

She had a million questions she wanted to ask him— What was he doing at the party last weekend? How did he know Donna and Frank? What did he do?—but her mouth was dry, and her voice had apparently deserted her as they made their way down the front walk to the silver pickup parked in the drive.

At the passenger door, she finally found her voice and turned to him as he pulled it open.

"So, how did you find me?"

This time his grin was a bit sheepish and, therefore, all the more disarming. He nodded for her to climb into the truck and then, thankfully, he offered her a hand. The dress and the shoes weren't her usual date attire, so she slipped her hand in his and let him boost her up to the seat. She dragged her eyes down over his face—five o'clock shadow darkened his jaws and neck and made her mouth water. He was still holding her hand, so she lowered her gaze to his long fingers wrapped around hers, the corded muscles and tendons in his forearm.

"I asked Donna." He gave her hand a gentle squeeze before letting go and then swung her door closed and loped around the front of the truck and settled in the driver's seat.

"Donna knew me?"

He chuckled as he started the truck.

"Well. You guys signed in for your passports, right?"

"Yes."

Asher fiddled with the stereo and looked at her in askance when Mumford and Sons played quietly around them. She nodded her agreement as he dropped the truck into drive and eased away from the curb.

"Okay. Donna remembered that you were with Whitney. She found your name on the list. And I Googled you."

"You Googled me?" She drew back in shock. "Are you kidding me?"

"White pages. Phone number look up." He shrugged.

"Mmm." She nodded. "Okay."

"Why? What else would I find under Leslie Brewer on Google?"

"Beats me," she answered with a laugh.

"Donna said she knows Whitney, but she'd never met you before."

"No. Whitney worked with Donna at the bank." Leslie wondered how much she was supposed to say in regards to Donna and the bank and the party. After all, she and Asher had both been there, and they had both seen some things. Done some things. Some steamy things. Things better left in the vault. "And Whitney and I have been friends since we were little kids."

Asher nodded, but his thick, dark eyebrows were drawn down in a deep frown. Should she ask if something was wrong? Her belly flipflopped with a stroke of nerves. Who was this man beside her? She'd been intimate with him, but she knew nothing about him. And yet, she wanted to know everything. Her body was on alert, her skin so sensitive that her dress rubbed uncomfortably over her legs and her stomach. She straightened quickly when she realized she was actually leaning toward him, like a plant seeking the sun.

"So, Whitney knows the bride?" He glanced at her, eyebrows cocked curiously, and then looked back at the road.

"Yes."

"You were Whitney's date."

A laugh rumbled deep inside her. Had he seen that kiss? Was he tiptoeing around that? Wondering if she and Whitney were a thing? Or if they'd had a thing?

Amused by his curiosity, wondering if the idea turned him on, she crossed her legs and let the hem of her dress slide up her thigh. Maybe she would let him wonder for a while.

"Yeah. Well, it was either that or sit at home and read." She shrugged and looked at him with a smile she hoped was sexy and mysterious. "Now she owes me."

"Nobody likes wedding showers," he mumbled.

"Well." She nibbled on her lower lip. It was true; she'd

been to a lot of showers through the years, starting back when she was a kid, going to bridal and baby showers for her cousins. Nobody got too excited about those invitations. "Everyone hates the stupid games."

Asher's warm, rich laughter filled the cab of the truck.

"Yeah? What kind of games?"

"Nothing like those at Donna and Frank's, I promise." She laughed with him. "The one I always hated was a memory game. If it was a bridal shower, someone would walk around the tables with a cookie sheet covered with all kinds of items. A safety pin. A bottle of aspirin. A teaspoon. Measuring cup. You name it. And then that person would leave the room, and you had to write down as many things as you could remember."

"Hmm." He nodded thoughtfully, but he drove for a few moments in quiet, eyes on the road. Leslie took advantage of the opportunity to study him. He was dressed in jeans again, and Leslie looked her fill, ready to share with Whitney. The faded, well-worn denim cupped his thighs and his groin like a lover's hands.

Leslie fisted her fingers and breathed deeply.

He wore a navy v-neck t-shirt, and Leslie saw that she had remembered correctly the way his shoulders and chest and thick arms stretched the material. He was thick and wide, and again, Leslie's gaze moved down over his middle to his groin.

She gulped for air again, suddenly feeling a bit flushed.

"Okay, so...." When he spoke, she jumped, afraid she was busted for ogling his body, most specifically the apex of his thighs, the fit of his snug jeans over what she was damned sure would be an impressive package. The memory of his arousal pressing into her belly threatened to overheat her again.

Her eyes flew to meet his, her cheeks still warm with thoughts of his body.

"The memory game." Either he didn't notice her body was smoking with sexual thoughts or he was going to give her a pass—she wasn't sure she liked either possibility—but he pursed his lips as he studied her face for a second. Leslie held her breath until he looked back to the windshield.

Rockfield wasn't big-city, like Chicago or even Springfield, but it wasn't farm country, either. However, Monday evenings weren't terribly crazy for traffic or crowds. Asher steered the truck with a casual wrist draped over the wheel. Leslie saw that they were at 30th and Maine and, therefore nearing Rossi's, a trendy, upscale Italian restaurant known for delicious food, good wine, and a pleasant, private dining experience.

"You were wearing a light blue blouse," he started. "And cute little heels. You looked a little terrified when you walked in, but you and your date went straight to Bronson in the back yard. You both did a shot, though I'm not sure what it was. You came strolling back into the house with martinis. And you joined the *Spin the Bottle* game as it was about to start."

Leslie stared at him silently, stunned because he'd noticed her long before she noticed him and because he was dead-on with the details so far.

"Whitney spun the bottle first, and you found yourself in the circle with her. Thank God she rolled a one, because the two of you in the center of that circle were fucking dynamite. Wasn't even so much the tongue-kissing, but the fact that you obviously knew each other intimately."

Leslie swallowed hard. His words were like warm velvet over her bare skin—now chilled when a moment ago, she'd been on fire. He'd watched her, all right. The idea that she and Whitney had turned him on was intriguing, and his use of the word *fucking* when he didn't really know her made her wet with desire.

"How'm I doing?" He shot her a grin.

Leslie worked her mouth to answer him, but she wasn't sure what to say. She considered unbuckling her seatbelt and sliding over to straddle him. Pressing that part of her body that ached again for his touch against his well-worn jeans.

"Who says tongue-kissing?" Her voice was soft and breathy. Asher shot her a look, hungry eyes eating her up before swinging back to the road.

"Well, I do, when I talk about you in that circle. I watched you slide your tongue against hers, and I felt it all over my skin."

Her lips formed a perfect O, but she only blinked at him.

"Once that kiss was over, you got a break. And then you got Craig Chase. Craig's an okay guy, I guess, but when you were in the circle with him and he had his mouth on yours, I kind of wanted to rip his fucking tongue out of his head and jam it down his throat."

A surprised laugh escaped her lips, so Leslie covered her mouth with her hand.

"I had to get a drink," he continued. "Felt like the damned house was on fire. I thought my dick was gonna explode before you called it quits."

Leslie thought the cab of the truck must be heading down Maine in flames. A vicious heat flooded her neck and her face, but a different kind of heat burned in her belly and between her thighs. Her skin prickled with awareness, and she figured he was looking at her again, though she refused to look and see.

"Imagine my surprise when you wandered outside later and talked to me."

Leslie chuckled nervously. "Wow." She straightened in her

seat when Asher turned into the parking lot and coasted to a stop in a space far from the door.

"And all you were gonna give me was a sweet little kiss and a poker chip."

Uncertain how to respond, she snuck a peek at him and then laughed and ducked her face to her hands when she saw the warm, ornery grin on his face.

"You smelled all girly and flowery, and your lips were soft and warm, and I was glad I got one kiss, at least." He shrugged as he cut the engine. He tugged the keys from the ignition and sat with his hand on his knee, eyes on her for a moment.

"I wanted to check on Whitney."

He nodded. "I get it. I'm glad you trusted me."

Leslie stared at him silently, still no idea what to say or what to think about the night so far.

"When I told you she was safe," he told her. "Frank and Donna run a tight ship. No one gets hurt at their parties."

Leslie answered with a slow nod, distracted by the flicker of pure, sexual energy in Asher's eyes.

"Good to know." This time, her words were a whisper.

He moved, but instead of opening his door to get out, Asher reached for her. She moaned softly when his gentle fingers cupped her chin. Their eyes met, and though the raw intimacy sent a hot spike of nerves through her lungs and into her belly, Leslie couldn't bear to look away.

Drunk on deep green eyes, Leslie felt a ripple of desire down to her toes. He leaned in closer, still, until she could feel his breath on her lips. Desperate to reach out and tangle her fingers in his longish hair—loose and silken tonight—she curled them into fists in her lap. Let her eyelids flutter closed when he kissed her, his lips soft but firm against hers.

This kiss was much like the first one at the party. Soft and chaste. Didn't feel like a down and dirty sex in the cab of the truck kind of kiss. But the night was still young, and Leslie had nowhere else she needed or wanted to be.

The fingers that held her chin moved slow but steady over her neck and then up over her cheek. Eyes closed, she waited and hoped for more. His lips teased hers again with that butterfly touch and then he kissed the corner of her mouth and nestled his lips—the five-o'clock shadow a little rough on her skin—under her lips and under her chin and over her neck.

It was sexy and sensual, and Leslie remembered his lips, the scruff on his face on other parts of her body. She clenched her core and squeezed her hands and moved her head, tipped it just enough to catch his lips with hers. She wanted his tongue; she wanted to taste him again.

She could think of nothing else now that he had kissed her. Now that she knew he had watched her slide her tongue over someone else's during the party games.

Lips parted now, he kissed her again. Soft and tender, his inner lips on hers, his teeth grazing her sensitive skin. Want for more, need for more, shot from her lips to her nipples, and Leslie moaned softly when she felt them grow hard in the lace bra under her dress.

"Kiss me." She finally lifted her hand, but rather than shove her fingers back through his hair, she framed his face with her fingers and licked his upper lip. She had meant to draw him in, to entice him into a deeper, more intimate kiss, but the move hit her like an open flame.

"I'm glad you trusted me. To pleasure you." His gruff whisper touched her lips and chased a chill of want up her spine. Because she needed to look at him, see his angelic face again—the hard-angled jaw and the curve of his thick, dark brows—she opened her eyes to drink him in. Mouths together, lips rubbing together gently, he startled her when he blinked his eyes open to look at her.

"None of that matters." He cocked an eyebrow and rested his forehead against hers. "The party. The games. What I watched you do. Just know it turned me on and licking you like I did and making you come was incredible. I've had blue fucking balls for three days, and I've spent those days thinking about all the dirty, sexy things I want to do to your body."

Mouth dry, eyes locked with his, she simply nodded.

"Do you want me to do dirty, sexy things to your body?"

"I do." She smoothed the palm of her hand over his cheek and then combed her fingers back through his hair. "I want to do every dirty, sexy thing with you."

He kissed her then. Forehead still pressed to hers, it was lazy and slow and lingering and then suddenly, he lunged, and the warm, velvet of his tongue stroked hers and Leslie felt it everywhere. Her nerve-endings were open and reaching for more, and she kissed him back, greedily licking his tongue and his lips and the cleft in his chin when he broke the kiss.

"First, though." He tipped his head and smiled that slow, sexy grin that seemed to be connected to her belly, the way it tipped up and hovered sideways inside her.

"What?"

"We're going to have dinner." He lifted his hand and traced his thumb over her lips, still wet from his kiss. "I'm going to watch you enjoy a meal, and I fucking hope you enjoy food the way you liked me kissing you. I'm going to watch your lips on a wineglass, and I'm going to kiss you again and taste that wine on your lips and your tongue."

Leslie wished she was staring at him with a come-hither look, but she was probably gaping. Sure, she'd had sex, but she'd never had it laid out before what a man planned to do with her body. The way Asher looked at her, the idea that he had fantasized and planned what he would do to her, where he would touch her made the ache between her legs unbearable.

"And then I'll kiss you here." He fluttered his fingertips over her throat. "And here."

She sucked in a sharp breath when he flicked her nipple through her dress. She met his eyes boldly, ready to suggest they skip dinner.

"Ready?" He drew back and offered her a small smile.

Her laugh was thick and sultry. Embarrassed by how badly she wanted him to take her here in the cab of the truck, with the evening sunlight bending through the windows and the possibility of an audience, she ducked her head to rest on his shoulder.

"You okay?"

She nodded and squeezed her eyes closed when he lifted a lock of her hair from her shoulder.

"Don't be embarrassed, Leslie," he murmured, his lips grazing her ear. "We'll get to that. First, we need to fuel our bodies."

She laughed out loud again and nodded when he pushed her away gently to look at her face. He gave her a quick peck on the cheek and then kissed her forehead, and warmth of a different kind flooded her body.

10

"So, what do you do at Hardin Landscaping?"

Completely taken aback by how Asher had gone from revved up and hot as Hades to civilized conversationalist in less than five minutes, Leslie blinked at him over the top of her menu. Lest he decide she was slow or just boring, she managed to bite her tongue before saying *huh* or *whaaat?*

"I'm..." She cleared her throat. The same eyes that had watched her like a predator just moments ago, and then caressed her like a lover, were now warm with genuine interest. She flicked her gaze lower, over his lips that were definitely kissable, and down over the dark scruff on his neck. "I kind of run the office." She zeroed in on the hollow at the base of Asher's throat. Decided she'd very much like to ring the hollow with the tip of her tongue and then suck on his skin there and draw it into her mouth. "I take care of customer relations and part orders and inventory."

When she raised her gaze to meet his, she found him smiling, obviously amused at her intimate survey.

"I help with ad campaigns, too," she added weakly, determined to get her head out of the gutter. Or Asher's clothes, actually. "I have a business degree. Studied some graphic design, too."

Asher started to speak, but when their waiter approached the table, he turned his attention away from her. They had discussed wine already, so he asked for a bottle of Sangiovese. Leslie was more knowledgeable about beer, as in she knew what she liked and where to get it and the average price for a twelve-pack. She didn't dislike wine, but there wasn't a lot of opportunity in her everyday life to sip bold, dry reds or crisp, chilled whites.

Maybe now she would find a reason, she decided when Asher handed the wine list back to the waiter. She decided on ravioli for dinner and set her menu aside.

"Do you enjoy it?" He looked over his menu one more time and stacked it on hers.

"My job?" When Asher nodded, Leslie smiled. "I do, yeah. I like the work. And I know the Hardins personally."

"Oh?" Asher quirked an eyebrow at her.

"I went to school with Jace Hardin."

"I don't know him," he said after a few moments.

"He's the youngest of the Hardin brothers," she explained. "Just got married last fall."

"Did you date him?"

Leslie laughed ruefully. "We tried."

"Didn't work out?"

"We're good friends." She shrugged. "It was like kissing my brother."

"So, your date included kissing?"

"It was one date." She wagged her eyebrows and laughed softly. "We went to dinner. Saw a movie. Shoulda known the kiss wasn't gonna be good, because we couldn't even hold hands. We talked all night. No awkward silences or anything. But just...no..." She pursed her lips and shook her head. "No physical attraction. He walked me up to my door.

Kissed me. He tried—we tried. But there was just nothing there."

Asher's lips twitched as he considered what she had said. "We've probably all had dates like that."

The waiter returned with their wine, and Leslie watched —a little bit fascinated—as he splashed a bit in a glass and handed it to Asher to taste. Her eyes were drawn to his sharp, angular cheekbones, but when he sipped the wine, she couldn't help but watch his lips on the glass, his Adam's apple when he swallowed. Asher nodded his approval, the waiter poured a glass for Leslie, and Asher waited for her to take a drink before he took another.

"So." She started to speak, because she had questions of her own, but Asher held up a finger to stop her.

"One more question?" He sounded both apologetic and hopeful. She nodded and sipped her wine again. Maybe she needed to learn a bit more about wine and drink it more often. Especially if that meant spending more time with Asher. "Are you seeing anyone?"

Leslie stared at him silently for a long moment.

"Of course not."

"Good."

She huffed out a quick breath, but the butterflies still fluttered in her belly. Shouldn't she ask the same of him? Shouldn't she confirm that he wasn't married? Just because his ring finger was bare, just because he'd performed oral sex on her and then called her and asked her to dinner didn't mean anything these days.

"How do you know Donna?" she finally asked. Because she had to know. No, he hadn't been carrying a passport at the party last weekend, so he hadn't been playing any sexy games. But that didn't mean he never had before. He seemed to know a lot about Donna and Frank and their elitist parties.

"Donna is my aunt." He leaned back in his chair and tossed his hands up as if to say *there you have it*.

"Your aunt?" Leslie repeated. She trilled a sharp note of laughter and then looked around the restaurant. The candles on the tables and the low-lighting from the sconces on the walls afforded them intimacy and privacy. Leslie was relieved no one was watching them.

"Yep." He raised his eyebrows and shrugged helplessly. "My mom's younger sister. I see my mom a lot, but Donna and I are pretty close, too."

Leslie stared at Asher silently, stunned that Donna Jackson was his aunt. That he'd dropped to his knees in front of her and put his mouth on her in his aunt's yard. That he was at a sex party his aunt and uncle had thrown. And that he apparently was well-acquainted with said parties and some of the party-goers.

"Wow." She nodded finally and reached for her wine.

"Is that okay?"

"Why wouldn't it be okay?" she asked, surprised to sound cool and collected. But Asher grinned when she gulped her wine, and she realized she'd given away her unease with the situation.

"What do you want to know? Ask me anything."

She wanted to know if his mom knew about the parties, but that was ridiculous. He was a grown man, and she wasn't sure she wanted an answer to that question, anyway. What if his parents were into…wild, uninhibited sexual fun, too? She wanted to be certain that Donna and Frank didn't participate in their party games, because the idea of Asher seeing his aunt doing…things…made her queasy. Did he go to a lot of the parties? Did he ever play the games?

Tongue tied, she simply stared at him and worked her mouth, unable to make a sound.

"Leslie."

She sighed and laughed and then gave herself a mental shake.

"Do Donna and Frank ever—?"

"No." He shook his head. "Their friends host parties, sometimes, and I think." He shrugged and grinned, and Leslie was relieved to see a twinge of pink in his cheeks. "They get into it, but not at their house. It's like a group thing. When they host, they walk the line."

"Mm-kay." She nodded.

"I have no interest in watching my aunt and uncle get dirty in *Spin the Bottle* or lose playing strip poker."

She laughed softly.

"And, no, I wasn't raised that way. My mom has no idea what kinds of things Donna does."

"Do you go to their parties often?"

"They invited me once. A few years ago. I think they had their eyes on some woman, thought they could set us up. She was nice enough. Played some games with her, but no, to answer your question." He tipped his head at her. "Nothing beyond a kiss and some dirty words."

"But you were there last weekend?"

"I'm a freelance journalist, so I'm on the road a lot. I have an apartment in Chicago. But I'm rarely there. When I'm in town, I stay at their place. I've managed to show up for party nights a time or two."

"That's…" She shook her head and shrugged and finally heaved another deep breath. "That's so beyond my wildest imagination."

"I've never enjoyed their parties as much as I did last weekend."

His intense gaze burned through her, and her nipples stood at attention again, as if he could see them.

"I wasn't supposed to go," she said softly. "Whitney called me right before the shower and begged me to go with her."

She snorted and rolled her eyes. "She had no idea what kind of shower it was going to be."

"Most people don't before they actually go to something at their house."

"Whit's boyfriend was out of town, so I went."

"So, you guys are just friends?"

"Yeah." She nodded. "I've never kissed a girl before Saturday night."

"And?"

"She's my best friend." She shrugged.

"It was pretty smokin' hot," he tossed out as he leaned back in the booth. Leslie looked up as the waiter returned to take their orders. Her pulse thrummed in her ears as she asked for the ravioli plate and Asher ordered scallops and fettucine. When the waiter walked away, Leslie sipped her wine, hoping Asher had forgotten that they were talking about her and Whitney. "Did you like it?"

"Well. No." She frowned and laughed again. "I mean, it was okay, but it was just weird. Not something I ever plan to do again."

"What about the guy you gave your poker chip to?" He leaned forward and rested his elbows on the table. "Did you like him?"

"That's not all I gave him." She arched an eyebrow, hoping to be sexy. But the gob smacked look on his face only turned her on more.

"What would you say if I told you I have your panties in my pocket right now?"

Her mouth was bone dry again, and wet heat pooled between her legs.

"Do you?"

The corner of his mouth tipped up.

"I haven't tasted anything as delicious as you since that

night." He reached for his glass and twisted it in a slow circle on the tabletop.

Leslie watched his thumb rub back and forth and back and forth over the bowl of the glass, the swirl of the red wine. She lifted her eyes to meet his gaze and was flooded with warmth. Desire.

"You stayed at their house that night?"

"Mmm." He nodded. "I did. The room I stay in is in the basement."

"Did anyone join you?"

"No." He shook his head. "I drank that beer you saw me get. And I stood to the side and watched you with your friend, long enough that I figured you decided I was a pervert. And then when you left, I went downstairs, locked my bedroom door, peeled my clothes off, and took a long, hot shower."

Leslie found it hard to breathe suddenly.

"I thought about you. Jerked off. Came so hard, it's a good thing they had music going, or they might have heard me. I didn't even know your name, so I couldn't say it, but you better believe I was thinking about your pussy clamped around my cock."

Skin on fire, Leslie peeked around the restaurant again. Several tables were filled around them, but those tables were all deeply involved in their own conversations, and Asher spoke quietly enough that it seemed impossible anyone would hear him.

She met his gaze again, the heat in his eyes searing her.

"Did you? Think about me?"

She nodded.

"Touch yourself?"

"Oh God." She sighed and rubbed her forehead with her fingertips. "I stayed at Whitney's that night. She was upset. She and her boyfriend broke up right before he left on a boys' trip. I thought about you, but it felt wrong to touch myself in her spare bedroom."

"The next night?" He sounded hopeful.

"Yes."

"I broke the rules and asked Donna who you were. Didn't tell her why I asked."

"I mentioned you to Whitney, but she didn't know you. Tried to tell myself it wasn't that kind of party."

"What do you mean?"

"I kind of doubt most guests at that party were looking for a follow up date kind of thing. I figured I should just enjoy the memory."

"So, it's okay that I called you?"

"Yes."

"You asked Whitney about me." He plucked his glass up to drink from it. "Did you tell her why?"

"No."

"No?" He drew back, as if her answer surprised him. "Don't girls share things like that?"

"We do." She grinned. "And I will. But not yet."

"Why's that?"

"I'm gonna be totally selfish with this. Sharing it with anyone too soon might take the thrill out of it."

"I could put the thrill back in you."

"Oh, I hope you do."

When he set his glass down, he reached over the table and stroked his fingers over the back of her hand.

"I told you what I plan to do to you after dinner."

She stared at him boldly and nodded without flinching.

"I'm gonna fuck you, Leslie Brewer. Over and over and over again until you can't walk tomorrow."

"I'm ready, Asher." She turned her hand over and linked her fingers with his.

Dinner was both agonizing and delicious. Agonizing because as much as Leslie enjoyed the food and the wine and especially the conversation, she couldn't look at him without feeling the current in the air. His eyes were bold and greedy, seeking eye contact and drilling into her heart and soul when she allowed him to, so she would drop her gaze to his lips. And remember the taste of his beer, of her own arousal and then, eyes still on his lips, his promise melted through her again, that he wanted to fuck her.

No man had ever looked her in the eye over a fancy dinner table with a fancy linen cloth and a lit candle and expensive wine and announced that he was going to fuck her. With anyone else, it might have offended her, made her angry. But his words, delivered in that deep sexy tone out of the mouth that had already driven her over the edge not once but twice, made her fidgety and anxious to escape the confines of civilization.

At the moment, she'd rather be flush against the wall of his aunt's garage with her jeans around her knees and his face between her legs than having dinner at Rossi's. Maybe if they saw each other enough, that crazed sexual need she had for him would fade and she could enjoy normal things like dinner and a fun conversation.

"You're thinking about it, aren't you?" he asked when their waiter took their dinner plates away. She'd struggled, but she'd eaten at least half of her dinner. Nerves and excitement kept her from overdoing it, but she decided she didn't want to be skin to skin with Asher and have her stomach growling, either.

Her eyes flew up to meet his gaze now. He wore that grin —the same one he'd worn last weekend when he'd compared her wimpy goodnight kiss to the kissing he'd watched her do earlier in the night.

"I am." She flashed him a grin and reveled in the way her honest answer hit him. He cleared his throat and laughed softly.

He'd told her he was twenty-nine, which worked well with her twenty-six, soon to be twenty-seven. He had talked about his two sisters and one brother, and he'd even laughed and told her that if he ever found out a guy had done to either of his sisters what he'd done to her at the shower, he'd rip his head off. Hiding her impish grin behind her glass, she clicked her tongue and when he tipped his head in askance, she simply mumbled that she'd bet his sisters would very much like to be in the position she was in last weekend with someone other than him.

Leslie talked about her older sister, and slipped in the fact that she was married, but she'd bet that her sister would also like to find herself in a situation like Leslie had last weekend. Asher's grin grew from sheepish to cocky, and Leslie decided she wanted to taste both of those smiles again.

They shared a love for movies, and they both agreed that slasher films were the most fun, though she also liked 80s movies and he liked cowboy movies. Asher told her he liked classic rock, and she said it depended on her mood.

Which sent her in a tailspin and right back to painfully aroused and wet.

When the waiter came back to check on them, Leslie nearly sobbed in relief. And yet, Asher ordered chocolate lava cake to share with her. He picked up the nearly empty wine bottle and eyed it for a moment. Leslie held her breath, afraid that he would order another. Maybe on a different night, she would happily sit here with him and drink another bottle, but tonight, she was desperate to be alone with him.

Asher chuckled when the waiter left to get their dessert.

"You're torturing me." She leaned over the table and shot him a frown.

"If you had any idea how sexy it is to see that desire in your eyes, you'd do it, too."

She huffed and laughed and then reached over the table to touch his hand.

"I thought you had blue balls, Asher," she said sweetly. "I can take care of that for you."

This time, her words got to him as she intended them to. He squirmed on his side of the booth, and his face twisted in a tight grimace.

"That's hitting below the belt."

"I want to get below your belt," she mumbled. Asher laughed, and then despite the flames of embarrassment in her cheeks, she laughed, too.

"We could take the cake to go." He pursed his lips. "I could smear the lava all over you and lick it off."

"Save some for me." She shrugged an eyebrow. "I want to lick you from your delicious shoulders down to your feet."

"Are you always so bold?" he asked with a grin.

"No. I'm not. At all." She laughed and waved her hands at her warm face. "But you're killing me. I want you."

As badly as Leslie wanted to join him on his side of the booth and straddle him and press her body against his, she wasn't a seductress. She settled for sharing the chocolate lava cake when it was served, greedily licking the melted chocolate from his fork when Asher fed it to her. The wine was good with the chocolate, but since Asher had mentioned licking it from her body, the idea was stuck in her head, and every time she watched him slide the fork in his mouth, she squirmed uncomfortably in her seat.

Finally, with a few bites of the cake left on the plate and the wine bottle empty, the waiter brought their bill and Asher tossed down a credit card.

"At the risk of sounding presumptuous." He tipped his head and studied her when the waiter took the black leather folder to process the payment. "Donna and Frank have a loft apartment in uptown Rockfield. They only stay there when they've been out late and had enough to drink, they aren't comfortable driving back out to Wild Canyon Estates."

Leslie licked her lips. He was asking her where she wanted to go. Where she wanted to be when he fucked her. Suddenly a bit shy, she lowered her gaze to the table. She'd be happy to shove the cake plate to the floor, climb on the table, and pull her dress up to fuck him right there. But she couldn't just say that out loud. She suspected that Donna's loft was trendy and rambling, decorated in marbles and granites and expensive art—like her home. Sex with him in a place like that, after a fancy night out like this, might feel staged. She didn't want to feel pressured to enjoy it or pressured to perform, and besides, she could also simply invite him to her house, her bedroom.

"Leslie?" he murmured as he leaned over the table. "Babe? Are you okay?"

A smile pulled at her lips as she gave him a small nod.

"We don't have to—"

She shook her head quickly, worried that he would misunderstand her reluctance. Feeling silly and childish, she couldn't admit to him that the thought of having sex in an uptown loft with expensive furnishings and marble flooring intimidated her.

"I'm just sitting here thinking that it feels weird to go back to your aunt's apartment with you. Like we're kids—"

"We don't have to, but I refuse to take you to their house and smuggle you downstairs."

"And in the same breath, I'm thinking why not clear the table and start now."

Asher threw his head back and laughed. Where the evening had been somewhat intimidating—the fancy restaurant, the wine, and the conversation, both sexy and normal—that laugh warmed her and reminded her that the first time she'd seen Asher, he'd been dressed in jeans and a tee, carrying a bottled beer. Still, even with the jeans and tee tonight, the atmosphere made her nervous.

The laughter and the way he dropped his head back and exposed the cords of his neck and the flash of his perfect white teeth comforted her and turned her on. Again.

"I live alone," she told him.

"I would love to take you home and spend the night in your bed, Leslie. I want you to go to bed every night with me in your mind."

She pressed her lips together.

"I might be harder to forget if I fuck you in your own bed."

"I don't think I'm ever gonna forget you," she said quietly, ignoring the pang in her belly. His words seemed to confirm the fact that whatever they were doing was temporary. She wouldn't back out, because she'd spent the last three nights fantasizing about being with him. They were adults; she'd never been reckless until that moment with him outside at the wedding shower. She didn't regret it; the memory thrilled her every time she relived it. Even if it was only for a night, she wanted to claim that ecstasy with him again.

And if she ached for him when it was over and he was gone, she'd find a way to put herself back together and go on. Walking away now would be a bigger regret than spending the night in his arms and saying goodbye tomorrow.

"I didn't wanna invite myself to your house." His lopsided grin tugged at her heart; the sheepish look on his face suggested he might be a little nervous, too. Crazy. He'd already claimed her physically. Didn't he know she was his for the taking, as long as he wanted her?

She said a silent prayer of thanks to Whitney for straightening up her bedroom. Making sure the bed was accessible if needed. The waiter returned with Asher's copy of the bill, asked if there was anything else he could get for them, and wished them a goodnight when Asher said no.

"Are we ready?" Asher turned to her when they were alone again. Leslie eyed the bit of cake still on the plate and nodded. His greedy eyes watched as she dipped her finger in the cooling chocolate center and then popped it in her mouth and sucked the chocolate off.

Asher rested his hand on her lower back as she stepped away from the booth. But as they walked, Leslie was surprised and thrilled when he took her hand in his. She liked holding hands in a relationship, and even though this didn't technically qualify as a relationship, she liked that it felt like it just for now.

The sky was painted in vivid purple, pink, and orange when they crossed the parking lot. Leslie sighed with contentment and then wondered if it was her imagination or if Asher had just squeezed her hand. At the passenger door of his truck, he took her other hand in his and stood toe to toe with her to kiss her. The simple, chaste kiss was possibly the most dangerous of all of the kisses he'd given her so far, because rather than passionate, it was tender. Rather than stroke anything low in her belly or between her legs, it touched her heart.

"I really wanted to bring that cake with us and eat it in bed." He pressed a kiss to her forehead and then backed away to open her door for her. Breathless with desire and heartache, Leslie stood for a moment and then finally climbed up into the truck.

"Get it together, Leslie." She smoothed her hands over her dress but stilled them in her lap when Asher pulled his door open and climbed into the driver's seat.

"Cats or dogs?" He started the truck, dropped it into gear, and glanced at her as he eased out of the parking spot.

"Um." She reached for her seatbelt and answered with a frown. "I don't have either, but dogs."

He nodded.

"Cake or pie?"

Her heart pounded up into her throat, and her lips twisted up in a grin.

"Cake, of course."

Asher roared with laughter.

"Ever done that?"

"Had cake in bed?"

"Has someone ever licked a food item off your body?"

Stunned by his direct question, she stared at him with wide eyes and flaming cheeks.

"No."

"Dammit. We definitely should have brought it with us."

"You've done this many times, I guess."

"A few." He shrugged. "It's okay." He gave her a lecherous grin. "I'm still gonna lick every inch of your body. And then I'm gonna suck on every inch of your body."

She wanted to ask him about the few times he'd licked

food items from female bodies, but if this was a one-night fling, she wasn't sure she wanted to know. She definitely didn't want to waste her time with him hearing about past sexual escapade.

"Leslie?" He rested his hand on her leg, his warm fingers sliding under the hem of her dress.

"Hmm?"

"I don't know what's going on in that head of yours, but I'm not some asshole guy who comes onto women at parties and goes down on them and then smears chocolate all over them to lick it off."

Leslie chuckled. She wanted to blow it off, but if he wasn't that guy, who was he?

"So, it wasn't you. It was me?" She grinned and tipped her head.

"It was definitely you," he agreed. "You were the prettiest —definitely the sexiest—woman at that party. When I kissed you, I didn't intend to end up with my mouth between your legs, but one taste wasn't enough."

"You don't have to do this," she said softly.

"Do what?"

"Sweet talk. Lie." She shrugged. "Whatever. I don't go to parties like that. And I haven't had sex in months, and I haven't had good sex in years, but I want this. I want to be with you tonight."

"Not lying." He shook his head. Leslie didn't know if he was arguing with her or making promises to her, and as she'd just told him, it didn't matter. She had been thinking about Asher since Friday night, and no matter what tomorrow would bring, she was going to enjoy whatever he wanted to do to her body.

The purple and pink and orange streaks in the sky hung lower and a shade darker when Asher pulled his truck into her short drive. He'd driven the rest of the way with his hand on her leg, and now, he gave her a gentle squeeze before climbing down from the truck and hurrying around to help her down. Except when she turned sideways, he didn't immediately help her out. Instead, he slipped both hands under the hem of her dress and molded his palms up over her thighs.

His eyes met hers with a challenge. Full dark hadn't yet fallen, and Leslie's neighbors were young and active, often outside. No one was around now, though, that she could tell, so she parted her legs slightly and gasped with delight when he rubbed his thumb over her clit. She felt the heat of his skin through the lace, but it wasn't enough. He leaned toward her and nuzzled her breasts with his face, his thumb moving in deliberately slow circles over the lace that covered her most sensitive skin.

"Asher." She said his name on a sigh, desperate to get inside her house and get their clothing out of the way.

"You're wet," he told her. "I bet you were wet when we were having dinner."

"I was," she agreed.

"Was it when I told you I wanted to fuck you? Over and over and over?"

She tugged at her lower lip when he pushed the lace aside and pushed his fingers inside her.

"Yes."

"Do you want me to fuck you?"

"Yes, please."

"Right here?"

She didn't want to move now, because he moved his fingers in and out, mimicking the sex act that she desperately needed.

"Leslie?"

"Inside."

"Are you worried about your neighbors?" He drew his

hand away so quickly, she mewled in protest and reached to stop him.

"No."

"Why inside then?" With his other hand, he cupped her breast.

"I wanna be naked, Asher. I want your skin on mine."

His lips claimed hers then, and before she could wiggle, slide further out of the seat, he touched her again, thrusting his fingers inside her and dragging them back over the magic spot he'd found last weekend.

"Asher," she moaned and tried to spread her legs further, hungry for more of him inside her. He added a third finger and then pressed her clit again with his thumb. Leslie screamed his name and tilted her hips up off the black leather seat.

"I love to make you come." He kissed a trail from her lips to a spot just below her ear.

"Come inside," she whispered. "Please. I want to touch you."

12

With Asher's help, she slid down his body, paralyzed when her heels hit the concrete drive. She held her breath for a moment, amazed to feel his chest heave with excitement against hers. His rapid breathing and his big cock pressed hard against her middle delighted her, so much that she wedged her hand between their bodies to cup his length.

"Fuck." He tugged her hand away, but he pressed an open-mouthed kiss on her cheek. "Let's go inside."

It crossed her mind to ask if he had condoms. She didn't. It had been so long since she'd been interested in anyone, she'd only bothered with birth control pills to regulate her period. Maybe he had a couple tucked away in his wallet, but the thought was a little disappointing after his announcement that he intended to fuck her over and over and over again.

Asher took her hand and pulled her from the v of the open truck door. She waited when he ducked his head in and opened the glove compartment. A rush of arousal flooded her when he pulled a small brown paper bag from the tiny compartment and then flipped it closed again.

"Just so you know I don't always keep a full box of condoms in my truck." He threw his arm around her shoulders and tugged her closer to drop a kiss on top of her head. "I got these before I picked you up."

She looked down when he pulled the receipt from the bag. The date and time stamp on the bottom of the paper showed that he had indeed purchased the condoms just before he picked her up for dinner. She grinned and dug her keys from her small purse so she could unlock the door.

The house was quiet, and considerably smaller than the house where she'd first seen him, and decorated with cute, comfortable items she liked but figured would never see the likes of Donna Jackson's house. But they were alone, and the second Asher pushed the door closed, she put her hands on his belt buckle.

"Whoa, whoa." He covered her hands with his and flashed that cute grin that made the skin around his eyes crinkle. "You first."

"You just did me," she argued.

"That was just a warm up." He shook his head and tugged her hands from his belt. "Where's your bedroom, Leslie?"

She turned her head in the direction of her room and started to answer him, but she yelped and laughed when he gathered the bottom of her dress in his hands and lifted it over her hips.

"Is this okay?" he asked when she looked back at him. "I wanna get you naked and get balls deep inside you, Leslie. But if you say no, I'll stop."

"I want you," she said simply. When he still hesitated, she took her dress in her hands. Nerves and arousal mixed in her belly, but she breathed deeply and then slipped the dress over her head and tossed it to the couch.

"You're beautiful." His greedy eyes roamed over her face

and then over her shoulders and her breasts in the pale blue lace. "I think I want these, too." He hooked his fingers in the waist of her panties and tugged her gently toward him.

With a laugh, she circled her arms around his neck. "If you keep it up, I'll have to go to work commando."

"While I love the thought of you walking around with no panties on, I don't love the thought of you working with a bunch of guys, with no panties on."

"Trust me." She flicked her tongue in the hollow of his neck. "No attraction. Feeling's mutual."

"Trust me." He moved his hands to cup her ass and hauled her up against him. "Guys who spend any time near you want you. You're pretty. You smell soft and sweet like flowers. You have a sexy laugh. And your lips look like they were made to be kissed."

"Is that poetry?" She tipped her head. "Someone I should know?"

"That's me." He leaned over to drop a peck on her lips. "A little over the moon for you."

"Show me."

He lifted her, just as he had in the yard by the garage the night of the party, and just as she had then, she wrapped her legs around his waist.

"Asher?" She buried her face in the crook of his neck.

"Hmm?"

"I'm so glad you found me."

She felt his laughter rumble in his chest. In her bedroom, rather than lay her down, he stood for a moment and smoothed his hands over her ass again. She hummed her appreciation when he slipped his fingers inside the crotch of her panties and rubbed his knuckles over her heat.

"You know what?" He turned his hand enough to press a finger inside her again.

"Hmm?"

"I don't love the thought of you wearing sexy-as-fuck lace underwear to work, either."

Her face still pressed to him, she smiled against his neck.

"Asher?"

"Leslie?"

"Fuck me."

He added another finger inside her, but she lifted her head to look him in the eyes.

"With this." She snaked her hand down between their bodies and rubbed her hand over his cock.

"You want it?"

"I do." She squeezed him again and unwound her legs from his waist when he loosened his hold on her. Starving for a taste of his skin, she fisted the hem of his t-shirt in her hands and pushed it up over smooth, hard abs that made her mouth water. He lifted his arms—her eyes followed the way his biceps bunched when he moved—and tugged the back of his shirt off over his head.

"Asher." She barely breathed his name as her hands moved without thought to sculpt his shoulders and his upper arms and then stroked down over his stomach. She moved closer to press a kiss to his chest, and her hands fumbled with his belt buckle.

He covered her hands with his and helped her pull his belt loose and then work the button and zipper of his jeans. Too hungry, too needy to wait, she moved her lips over his chest and sunk her teeth into his skin.

He hissed and bit off a string of smoking hot words when she sucked his hard, flat nipple into her mouth. Leslie shoved her hands inside his open jeans, slung low over his hips now, and cupped his ass cheeks.

"Come here." He caught her chin in his hand and held her still for a kiss. His tongue plunged deep and stroked hers in long, slow thrusts. Leslie moved her hands, sliding her fingers inside his boxer briefs. With a boldness foreign to her, she let her fingers roam around his perfect ass before molding her hands over his hips and around to cup his cock.

Again, Asher hissed, but he rocked into her hand and moaned long and low when she circled her fingers around his shaft.

"Take 'em off," she whispered. "Please."

He pulled her hands from his pants and brought them to his lips to kiss them. Leslie smoothed her fingertips over his mouth and his cheeks as he shoved his jeans and his briefs down and stepped out of them.

Before she could move, he swept her into his arms again and carried her across the room to the bed. When he laid her down, she reached for him with both hands. Asher knelt on the edge of the bed, head ducked, eyes on her hands as she stroked him from his balls to his head.

She'd done it before, touched a guy, sucked a guy, but she'd never *wanted, needed,* to get her mouth on a guy the way she needed to taste Asher. Worried that she wouldn't do it right, that he would get frustrated with her, she tipped her head up to look at him.

"Your hands on my cock feel so fuckin' good," he told her.

She leaned forward, her hands cupped around his balls, and flicked the tip of his cock with her tongue.

"Leslie."

"Let me taste you." She wrapped her arm around his waist and tugged him closer. He moaned and rocked into her again when she closed her lips around his head. Fingers wrapped around his shaft, she rubbed her thumb over his balls and up his length and took him in, the tip of his cock nearly at her throat.

She shivered when she felt his hand in her hair and then on her back. The elastic of her bra gave and reluctantly, she sat back and released him so he could drag the lace from her breasts. Electricity shot through her when he flicked her nipples.

This time, she licked a trail from his balls up his shaft to his head. His cock was thick and hard with arousal, and when she circled the tip with her tongue, she tasted a drop of pre-cum.

"I said you first," he reminded her. She laughed as he gently pushed her to lie back and hooked his fingers in her panties to take them off her. His intense gaze made her hot and needy, so she cupped her breasts in her hands to pinch her nipples with her fingertips.

He wasted no more time, his hands heavy on her thighs as he spread her open for his delight. She gasped when he fucked her with his fingers, but when he lowered his head to kiss her, she lifted her hips from the bed in offering. The familiar sensation of his fingers moving knowingly inside her and his lips tugging at her clit and his tongue licking and bathing her drove a wild shiver up her back. With one hand still on her breasts, she drove the fingers of the other into his hair and held on as the orgasm tore through her with an intensity that almost frightened her.

"Condoms," he mumbled when he lifted his head to look at her.

"There." She pointed to the brown bag where he'd dropped it on the nightstand moments ago when he'd carried her into her room. He knelt on the bed and twisted around to grab the bag. Leslie watched him tear the box open and grab a condom. She dipped her fingers into her wet folds as he tore the package open with his teeth.

"You're gonna kill me," he muttered when he realized she was touching herself. "But what a perfect way to go."

With a lazy grin, she lifted the same hand and stroked the length of his shaft.

"Nope. One more touch, and I'm gonna make a fool of myself." He laughed and pushed her hand away. Leslie raised up on her elbows to watch him roll the rubber over his length. "Are you sure?"

She laughed and tipped her head as she hooked her arm around his neck. Tasting herself on his mouth again was arousing, and she thrilled to the fact that this time, he was going to make love to her. His lips hovered near hers, and he settled his hands on her hips.

"I want you to fuck me." She nipped at his earlobe and then lay back as he eased himself inside her inch by inch until his balls were tucked up against her. He was long and thick and hard; Leslie—impatient to move with him—bent her knees and lifted her hips.

"Give me a second, babe. I'd like this to last a few minutes."

"You've got a whole box of condoms," she reminded him, her lips pressed to his ear.

"First impressions." He rubbed his lips over hers and opened his eyes to stare into hers.

"Let's talk about first impressions." She traced circles over his back. "Delicious-looking shoulders in a tight gray tee. Nice ass. A rakish ponytail and sexy green eyes. Flirty and fun, you turned my nice goodnight kiss and spun it on its ass. Backed me up against a wall, put your mouth on me, and made me come twice."

"Is all of this good?" He cocked an eyebrow at her and slowly pulled out of her.

"Oh yes, it's so fucking good." She nodded. "Then you found me. And asked me to dinner. Kissed me before dinner. Told me you were gonna fuck me. I was so aroused at Rossi's, I could have wiggled once or twice in the booth and come."

"Yeah?" His slow, deliberate thrust filled her completely and drew a long, soft moan of pleasure from her lips.

"And then, you made me come in the truck before you helped me out." Her sigh was a mix of longing and contentment when he dipped his head and plucked her nipple with his teeth.

"I shouldn't have done that?" He lifted his head and offered her the grin that turned her heart upside down.

"I love that you did that." She wrapped her legs around his waist and locked her ankles at his back. "And I love that you're doing me."

"Are you okay?" He rested his forehead on hers, pressing in and out with those tantalizingly slow strokes of his hips.

"Yes."

"I'm not hurting you?"

"I don't remember the last time something felt this good." She combed her fingers up through his hair and captured his mouth for a long, wet kiss. When Asher broke the kiss, he dipped his head to her neck and nipped at her, his hips pumping a bit faster and harder. Leslie moved her legs, slid them down around his and pushed the heels of her feet into the bed to move with him and meet him thrust for thrust.

"Les?" His gruff voice traced a chill over her skin.

"I'm close." She kept moving with him, but when he shifted the angle of his hips to give her more pressure on her clit, her body seized and her hips shot up high and hard. With her back arched, Asher took her nipples in his teeth one at a time, to bite her, and then lave them with his tongue and ease the stinging sensation. "I love what you do to my body," she whispered as she collapsed back to the bed. "I love your body, Asher." Her hands moved over his chest and his shoulders, her fingers hungry for his warm, hot skin and the sweat at his hairline. She moved with him in a steady rhythm, heart still pounding in her chest, as she concentrated on squeezing his cock inside her.

"You're beautiful." He pushed the words out through

clenched teeth as his body tensed over hers. Leslie smoothed her hands down over his arms and his belly and then curved them around his hips and sank her fingernails into his ass. "Babe, you're so fuckin' hot."

Asher eased out of her and then lowered himself to lay beside her. She turned to lay on her side and rested her hand on his chest.

"Are you really gonna stay with me tonight?" she whispered.

"Yes."

She lifted her head and draped herself over his chest to kiss him. Their tongues moved in the same rhythm their bodies had just moments before; Leslie threw her leg over his when he wrapped his arm around her.

"How many condoms are in that box?"

His laughter rumbled in his stomach, and she felt it in the palm of her hand as she smoothed it over his hot, sticky skin.

"I don't wanna hurt you." His voice was gruff, a little too serious. Mouth on his neck, Leslie drew back to study his face. "You'll be sore tomorrow."

She arched an eyebrow and shrugged. "It's a good sore."

His lips shot up in a quick grin, and he drew his hand down the length of her back.

"You tell me when you've had enough," he suggested.

"Mmm." She winced and shook her head. "I might just have to lock you up and keep you in my bed forever."

"I could deal with that." He stroked his fingers over her ass and gave her a gentle squeeze. "C'mere." He patted her ass and helped her move to straddle his hips. Leslie rubbed her clit over his cock, still at half-mast, and shivered with pleasure. "That feels good but come up here."

"What?" She laughed as he palmed the back of her thighs and tugged her further up his body. "What're you doing?"

Breathless, she whimpered with pleasure when he pulled her up to straddle his mouth.

"I love kissing you here." He grazed the sensitive skin of her inner thighs with his teeth and then dragged the scruff on his cheeks over the same spots. Before Leslie could react to that, he smoothed the pads of his thumbs over the chafed skin and licked her seam, focusing on her clit.

"Asher." She dropped her head back as he explored her folds with his tongue, careful to taste every inch of her. The light, playful strokes of his tongue were so different from the way he'd licked her before, with the heavy pressure and his only intention to make her come. Now, he explored her as if for his own enjoyment. His thumbs held her open, and he tilted her hips forward to thrust his tongue inside her pussy, again with light and playful strokes and jabs.

"Feel good?" He pressed his lips to her folds as he spoke, and the vibration of his voice tickled her.

"Yes."

"I like the way you taste. I like your heat. That you're wet."

"I like the soft strokes," she whispered. She rolled her head on her neck and looked down to watch him play between her legs.

"Better than the pressure?"

She laughed and shook her head. "Oh, no. Good, but not better."

"Do you want to come again?"

"I don't know if I can," she whispered.

"I need to get rid of this condom," he reminded her.

"Okay." She grinned, but she didn't shift away from him, so he continued to play between her legs. A knot of pressure grew again low and deep inside her. "Asher?"

"Do it." His eyes met hers as she dipped her fingers between her legs. The added pressure of her fingers on her clit to the still playful, light touch of his tongue drove her over the edge again. Asher's hands cupped her ass cheeks firmly as the streak of hot tingly pleasure shot through her. Head back, eyes closed, she realized Asher was now sucking on her fingers. Her body quivering with delight, she collapsed beside him again and rested her head on his shoulder.

13

"How often do you get to Chicago?"

Leslie blinked her eyes open, but she didn't answer Asher immediately. Instead, she focused on the soft caress of his hand on her bare back. They had moved, eventually. Asher had slipped into the bathroom to deal with the condom. Leslie had padded naked through the house to turn the lights off. They'd curled up together again under the covers and shared kisses and touches to explore and learn each other's bodies. Leslie had been thrilled to smooth her hands over his shoulders and memorize the hard muscles under his smooth, warm skin. Asher found her ticklish belly entertaining.

Though Leslie tried to fight it, she'd gone to sleep in his arms. He woke her after midnight, his hands molding her breasts. They'd made slow, sweet love. Leslie found that she loved his tender touches as much as she did his rough, crazed touches.

Even though she reminded herself of her vow—enjoy whatever Asher had to offer her—midnight had brought desperation gnawing at her belly and her heart, because daylight would take him from her. And they'd made no promises to each other, not even to talk again once this incredible night was over.

"Not often," she whispered.

"But sometimes?" He sounded hopeful.

"Maybe once a year," she mumbled. Not even that often, really. But maybe if he asked her to visit?

"Where do you stay? When you're in the city?"

Leslie stretched and buried her face in her pillow before turning over to face him. She couldn't see him in the darkness, but she felt his breath on her face and her body was pressed to his, shoulders to feet.

"Just." She sighed. "Hotels. I don't go much, Asher. The last time Whitney and I were there for a shopping weekend was before Christmas."

She felt a little guilty, even though she knew it was stupid. As much as she wanted this to be more than one night of incredible sex, odds were the attraction would fizzle for both of them after a few days passed. And even if it didn't, she had a life here, and it was a good one. She was happy. Love might inspire her to change something—like location and therefore a job—but sex, mind-blowing orgasms would not.

"Okay." The kiss he pressed to her forehead eased the guilt but not the wistfulness. She might not be ready to say it to Asher, but she could admit it to herself. She wanted more with him. She wanted the chance to spend time with him, to see if they were as compatible outside the bedroom as they were in it. "How do you feel about phone sex?"

She laughed softly.

"No, really. Do you text much? Are you one of those girls who likes to talk on the phone?"

"I text a lot. And talking just depends on who I'm talking to and what else is going on."

"So. When I head back, we could stay in contact?"

"Yeah." She lifted her hand and traced her fingertips over his cheekbone. "I'd like that."

"New-age pen pals."

"Wow. Okay."

"With benefits." He closed his fingers around her side, making her jump and yelp. A giggle slipped out before she sank her teeth into his neck.

"I don't sext," she told him.

"But maybe phone sex."

Before she could answer him, he claimed her lips in a long, slow kiss. His hand roamed possessively over her front, touching her most intimate parts as if reminding her the power he had over her body.

"Maybe."

"Well, that's something," he decided. "If I can't talk you into coming to Chicago with me."

"You freelance, so I'm guessing you travel a lot." He'd told her that, hadn't he?

"I do," he confessed. "But I like the idea of you being around my place some. The idea of me being on the road and you being in my apartment. Naked. In my bed."

"I can be naked in my bed. You can think about me that way."

"I know. Guess it sounds kind of Neanderthal of me to want you in my place for when I'm around."

It did. Kind of. But something about lounging around Asher's place, being there to greet him when he came home from a trip or even just at the end of a long day, tempted her. Leslie reminded herself that she'd been involved in other relationships that she'd invested more time and heart and soul in, and if those relationships hadn't worked out, surely what was going on between herself and Asher would fizzle out quickly.

Time to let that fantasy go and get back to the real world.

"How often are you here?"

"Um." He flopped over to lie on his back. He tugged her along with him, so that she was now propped to lie beside him. "More than you're in Chicago, I guess."

That thought thrilled her, but it also filled her with dread. What if he happened in on Donna and Frank's parties a lot? What if he hooked up with a new woman at every party? Maybe she had been stupid to assume their connection was special. So, he'd turned her inside out with an earth-shattering orgasm the first night they'd met. It had been a damned big deal for her. Maybe not for him.

"Yeah? Do you always stay at your aunt's house?"

"Mm-hmm." He stretched and lifted his arm up over his head. Leslie felt the change in his position. She took a moment to visualize the pop of his bicep and then ran her fingers over that spot, surprised her mouth wasn't actually watering. "I mean, they have a nice setup."

As much as his words hurt, she chuckled. Sadly, it sounded a bit like a sob to her own ears.

"I suppose they do." She lowered her head again and pressed her lips to his collarbone.

"What?" He stroked his hand up her side. Leslie sighed against his skin as he paused to caress her breast; her nipple beaded at the touch of his fingers.

"What's not to like for a single guy like you at a place like that?"

"Their basement is like an apartment. It's like I have my own place."

"Mmm." She nodded. "Sounds nice."

"Leslie." He tweaked her nipple before moving his hand. This time he cupped her chin in his fingers. "What's wrong?"

"Nothing." She shook her head, still resting on his shoulder. With her comforter shoved to the end of the bed and their feet tangled in the sheet, she was cold now. The thought of Asher taking a different party guest to his own little place in his aunt's basement lodged in her throat and made it hard to breathe.

It's okay, she reminded herself. One night. You vowed to enjoy one night with him. Whatever he does when he's not with you means nothing.

"Something," he argued. "Tell me what you're thinking."

He nudged her gently until she was lying on her back and then he slid a leg over her to straddle her hips. Rather than press his cock between her legs, though, he leaned forward to drop sweet, chaste kisses over her forehead and her nose.

"Is this a tactical move? Do you think you can kiss it out of me?"

"Isn't there a saying about love and war? It's all fair?"

"No love or war here," she said with a slow grin, "so, no. You can't do that."

"Really? You think that? There's no love here?"

"Isn't it a bit soon to think so?"

"So." Asher flicked his tongue over her the center of her top lip. "Leslie Brewer doesn't believe in love at first sight."

"I don't think so," she answered.

"Just lust at first sight." Here, he did grind his hips to hers, shocking her with his arousal again.

"Before you, I don't even know that I believed in lust at first sight," she whispered.

"You've never been attracted to someone with one look?"

"Attracted, yes." She parted her lips when he pressed his against them. Asher took a moment to plunder her mouth, his tongue sliding over her teeth and then curling around hers as if to claim it, claim her. "Drop-my-panties-and-spread-my-legs lust at first sight? No."

"Well, thank God for that." He kissed his way over her cheek to her ear and sucked gently on her lobe. "I'd hate to think you might find someone else to turn your head while I'm gone."

"What about you?" When she heard the fear in her gruff voice, she squeezed her eyes closed. So much for playing tonight cool, living in the moment. Leslie knew there were all kinds of people who simply weren't into monogamy or didn't care to be involved in relationships. She assumed there were even more of those people in Chicago, just because the population was so much bigger. Trying to claim him, to take more than what he was offering, would only turn him off. As it stood right now, it seemed he wanted to at least be friends. She didn't love the idea of being friends, of hearing any tales about his adventures with other women. But if he was off gallivanting all over the country or world, even, and she was happy here in her life, she wanted to stay in touch.

"What about—?" He stopped talking and lifted his face. Leslie figured he was staring, trying to see her in the darkness. He shifted over her, leaning way to the left. Leslie turned her head away as she realized he was going to turn the lamp on. She heard the tiny click of the switch and then a bit of golden lamp light fell across the bed. Asher's fingers still on her face, he turned her chin to force her to look at him. He grinned when their eyes met, his gaze warm and compassionate. "Hey."

"Hey."

"Remember me?" He wiggled his eyebrows.

She lifted her fingers to touch his lips and dragged her eyes down over his face. "I don't think I'm ever gonna forget you."

"I hope not." He spoke quietly, an urgency in his voice that nearly rendered her speechless. "What did you mean? What about me?"

"Never mind." She pressed his lips together. "Not important."

"I think it was important," he argued.

"How many women are you attracted to at first sight?"

His eyebrows shot up to his hairline.

"Leslie, I don't do this anymore than you."

"Have sex?"

"I've had girlfriends, and I've had a few really crazy short flings. But this...what I feel for you...how fast I felt all of it? That's all new."

"It is?" Her whisper sounded hopeful, and she gave herself another mental kick in the ass.

"Yes." He traced his fingertip over her nose and then leaned over to kiss the tip of her nose. "I was seeing someone. Around Christmas. We'd been together for a couple of months, but it fizzled out. No hard feelings, just no...feelings, really. I like sex, and I like women, but I'm not the guy who just moves from random hook up to random hook up."

"And what about Donna and Frank's?"

"I told you I don't play their games."

"No, but you're at the parties."

He shrugged. "But I don't participate."

"How many women do you get to kiss goodnight?"

"Just you," he said quietly. "You're the only woman I've watched every second, wishing that I was playing the damned games just so I could meet you. Get your name. Get my hands on you."

"Okay."

"I made that sound really horrible, didn't I?" He cringed. "That Donna and Frank have a really nice setup for me."

She grinned and shrugged her shoulders.

"Seems like the perfect setup for a guy like you." She lifted her hands and pressed them to his chest. "Hang around the party. Play if you want. Scope out who's there. Kiss someone goodnight. Take her downstairs for your own night of fun."

"A guy like me?" He shook his head. "What does that mean?"

"Young. Single. Smokin' hot to look at. Magic hands and mouth."

He sighed and shrugged. "Yeah, it does sound perfect. And I will admit that there have been parties where I've watched some stuff. Enjoyed watching some stuff. But I've never played the games and never wanted to. I was raised in a house with parents who loved each other. Not saying Donna and Frank don't. But my parents were different. They wouldn't dream of stuff like that. And I love Donna and Frank. They're good people."

Leslie rubbed her thumbs down over Asher's pecs and flicked his nipples with her nails. Asher hissed his appreciation.

"But I'd rather have the kind of thing my parents do."

She stared at him silently for a moment. Sure, he could be lying. But she wasn't sure what he would gain from it. She'd already climbed into bed with him. He'd given her so much more in the way of sexual satisfaction than any other lover ever had. Leslie hated the thought of being friends with benefits, but she liked him, and she loved his benefits, and if that's all he offered, she was all over it. He had to know that, too.

"Do Donna and Frank pressure you to do the games? To...try that lifestyle?"

"Never." He shook his head. "If I wanted to, I could hang out in the basement and watch a movie. Or go out for the night. They wouldn't have pressured you to carry a passport, either, if you had said no."

"Yeah, I wasn't aware that I could say no," she said with a grin. "But now, I'm kind of glad I did play. What if I wouldn't have had a poker chip to give you to kiss you?"

"Pretty sure I'd have used my excellent sleuthing skills to find you anyway."

"But I'd have missed out on the mind-blowing orgasms."

"True." He nodded.

"When do you have to leave?"

"Heading back to Chicago tomorrow."

He didn't want to go. She could read it in the slump of his shoulders and the downturn of his lips.

Leslie took a deep breath and wished for courage or indifference. "And when will you be back here?"

"Soon." He tipped his head. "But not soon enough."

"Six months?"

"A few weeks, tops. Sooner if I can manage it."

"Okay."

"Will you wait for me?" He arched his eyebrows hopefully. "Save all of you...the smiles and the laughter and your pretty pussy just for me?"

Leslie snorted and then laughed out loud.

"Yes."

"Will you have phone sex with me while I'm gone?"

"Maybe."

"But no sexting?"

"No."

"Kissy face emojis?"

She laughed again as she raised up and looped her arm around the back of Asher's neck.

"I could probably send some kissy face emojis," she whispered as she captured his earlobe in her teeth. "Are you gonna save that grin for me? The really cute, ornery grin that makes your eyes twinkle?"

"I wasn't aware I had that grin."

"Oh, you do. That's the grin you threw down right before you kissed me goodnight at the party."

"Mmm." He wiggled his eyebrows. "I will."

"And this?" She cupped her hand over his cock and rubbed her thumb over his head. "Will you save this for only me?"

"Yes."

"One more thing, Asher." She tugged him down to lie on top of her again. "Will you send me kissy faces, too?"

"Every night."

14

True to his word, Asher texted Leslie the following morning as soon as he was gone. They'd climbed out of her bed with her alarm; much too early after a night of loving and much too soon when Asher had to go back to his aunt's house and pack up to head back to his apartment in Chicago. Hot coffee, a hot shower, and hot shower sex—not necessarily in that order—helped to revive her, but once she was at work, her spirits sagged as much as her shoulders did.

The Hardin guys seemed to notice something was different about her. When that thought occurred to her, she laughed to herself, thankful that she had been able to walk into the building without looking like she'd been horseback riding all day and all night. But she was quiet, because she knew Asher's plan was to be on the road within an hour of leaving her place.

Her boss didn't question her, simply offered her the usual warm smile as he looked over the repair schedule for the shop. Jace, however, lingered in the front of the store, looking for all the world as if he wanted to poke the bear and ask some questions. Leslie wasn't sure how much she wanted to tell him. She certainly wouldn't go into any detail, whatsoever, but she wasn't sure she even wanted him to know she'd met someone. Even if she and Asher maintained any sort of friendship, it wasn't as if his path would ever cross with Jace Hardin's.

She and Whitney were meeting after work for drinks, where Leslie knew Whitney would pump her for every detail, right down to how many orgasms she'd had, the size of Asher's package, and if she planned or wanted to see him again. Again, not a conversation she would ever have with Jace Hardin or his brothers or dad.

"What's up with you today?" Jace propped his elbows on the counter in front of her and stared her down. She wasn't up for the dare, so she was relieved when she heard her phone buzz. Normally, she didn't even have it out at work, though no one cared if she did. Today, just because Asher was leaving, she wanted it close by. Just in case.

Not answering Jace, she palmed her phone and turned it over.

Three kissy face emojis. Heat flooded her face, and warmth spread through her chest, and an altogether different sort of heat hit her between her thighs. She attempted to bite back a smile, but it was obvious she failed when Jace ducked his head a bit to catch her eye and then wiggled his eyebrows when he did.

"Leslie?"

She made a mental note to ask Asher not to sext her at work—she'd refused to do that, but he had made no promises—just in case the whole damned Hardin Landscaping crew happened to be around. Quickly, Leslie fired off three kissy face emojis back at Asher and set her phone down.

"Yes?" She lifted her chin to look at Jace.

Asher had sent three kisses. Maybe she should have added

a couple. Five was a good number. Maybe only three looked like she was simply mimicking him. That she couldn't be bothered to add more. What if Asher didn't believe she was interested? After all, last night she'd told him she didn't believe in love at first sight. Still didn't—not really, even though she certainly wished she and Asher could explore their emotions the same as they had each other's bodies.

"You okay?"

"Yep."

When Jace simply stood there watching her still, she added an emphatic nod. Yep, indeedy. She was a-okay.

Five might have been too many, though. She didn't want to look like she was trying too hard. And it was so soon. Okay, they'd swapped some promises that they could maybe be friends with benefits or long-distance lovers or a little bit of something in between. But what if he'd been playing her? Five kissy face emojis might have given away the fact that she was all in, and maybe the prudent thing to do would be to wait a bit. Feel him out, rather than just up. See how Asher played things. It was entirely possible he'd fed her a line of bullshit just so he'd have a sure thing anytime he came here to see his aunt. And again, if that was the case, Leslie was all in. Except her heart. No need to drag her heart into anything.

"Because yesterday…" Jace drew that word out over ten seconds and then let it hang there between them. He lifted a shoulder and an eyebrow suggestively, but Leslie chose to play dumb.

"What about yesterday?" she finally asked when he didn't go on.

"Well. You got all jumpy and weird late in the day."

"I did?"

"You did." He nodded. "And a minute ago, you came in looking like someone kicked your dog."

"Don't have one."

Jace rolled his eyes. "Just go with me on this." She laughed softly and rolled her hand in a circular motion to tell him to continue. "And then two seconds ago, you just lit up like someone plugged you in."

Leslie studied him silently and finally drew in a deep breath.

"I'm good, Jace."

"So, it's a guy." He nodded.

"Why would you think that?"

"Am I wrong?"

"I don't know what it is," she mumbled, back to worrying about the kissy face emojis and the things she and Asher had said to each other through the night.

"Oh." Jace grinned. "I was just kind of gonna throw stuff at you until I got a reaction. You're pretty transparent, Brewer."

Leslie laughed, despite the ache in her chest. All of the misgivings would go away if he were here. She missed him. Already. It would be weeks, at least, before she saw him again, if not longer. She wasn't sure how she was going to handle any sort of long-distance relationship; she hadn't had any successful normal relationships to date.

"Okay." Jace drummed a little solo on the counter. "I won't hound you about it, because I'm guessing it's kind of new, whatever it is. Just wanted to make sure you're okay."

Touched by his concern, she nodded and thanked him as she wrapped her fingers around her mouse. Time to get to work. Their first repair customer would be strolling in soon.

Asher texted once an hour, but never on the hour. By the time quitting time rolled around and Leslie was climbing into her Rav 4 to meet Whitney at Lou's Bar for drinks, she'd racked up thirty-seven kissy face emojis. She laughed as she drove across town to Lou's, finding it funny that she had actually worried this morning about the number of kissy faces she sent back to him. He wasn't counting. No pattern to how many texts or emojis, as far as she could tell. Seemed like he was just firing them off when he thought of her.

That possibility warmed her from head to toe again. The texts didn't make the fact that she wasn't going to see Asher tonight any easier, but they'd taken the sharp sting out of missing him. She found Whitney at a high-top table in the far corner of the little bar they frequented for girls' nights. Lou herself was tending bar tonight, and the short, stout older woman bellowed a friendly hello to her. Leslie waved and called hello as she hustled over the worn wooden floor to join her friend.

"You look gorgeous!" She threw her arms around Whitney when she stood to greet her. "You and Shawn must have fixed everything."

"Proof that you had a fantastic night, because even though Shawn and I did fix everything, I look like hell from no sleep."

Leslie laughed as she climbed up to sit on the chair opposite Whitney.

"Why no sleep?"

"Don't change the subject on me." Whitney shook her head. She twisted her pint glass on the tabletop and batted her eyelashes at Leslie.

"No, seriously. You and Shawn? You're okay?"

"We're okay," Whitney promised. "We're the same as always, so yeah. Okay. But."

Leslie winced, wishing that things would progress for her friend and her boyfriend.

"No sleep because you had a night of wild and crazy sex?"

"No, I think that's you," Whitney argued in a syrupy sweet voice. "No sleep because even though we fixed things, I don't know if I'm happy. Last word on it. Tell. Me."

Leslie laughed as Lou approached their table.

"What're you drinkin' tonight?"

"Whatever Whit's having," Leslie answered. Lou nodded and turned to fetch the beer for her.

"So. Here's what I know. He has sexy-as-fuck broad shoulders and a ponytail. And his name is Asher Collins."

Leslie smacked her lips together and nodded. She opened her mouth to speak but lost her courage. What would Whitney say about the night of the shower? Leslie didn't believe she would judge her, but always before, they'd both been completely honest and open with each other. Even after college, when life got real and the girlfriend bond could have submitted to the husband and family thing, she and Whitney had told each other everything.

"Oh, Whitney." A hundred different emotions tainted her words and the sigh she let loose with them. Lou returned with her beer without ceremony. She thumped Leslie on the shoulder as she walked away, already talking to the patrons at the table behind them.

"Oh, Whitney…good? Or bad?"

"Oh, so good." Leslie propped her elbows on the table and scrubbed furiously at her flaming cheeks.

"Okay, well, I still want details. I'll never outgrow the need for details. You know that, right? Like, I want to know if he went left or right first. I need to know everything."

"Left or right?" Leslie tipped her head with a frown.

"Nipples." Whitney shrugged.

Leslie giggled. "Actually, he kind of went dead south so fast, I don't even know. Center, south, I guess."

"He—?" Whitney shook her head. "Come again?"

"I did."

"Leslie. Brewer." Whitney picked her beer up, but she simply held it for a moment. Eyes dancing with delight, she finally tossed her other hand up as if to ask what Leslie was waiting for.

"So." Leslie cleared her throat. She drummed her fingers on the table and swallowed hard. "I didn't tell you everything from the night of the shower."

"I figured." Whitney arched her brow and nodded. "So, tell me now."

"I just…wasn't…ready. Wasn't sure what to—"

"I get it. Tell me now."

"I gave him my poker chip," Leslie reminded her. Whitney finally took a drink and set her glass down.

"Right."

"He'd seen us playing *Spin the Bottle*, so he teased me when I kissed him."

"Too much tongue?" Whitney winked.

"Not enough when I kissed him." Leslie laughed softly.

"Hmm." Whitney nodded. "Okay. So, what did he do?"

"Kissed me. A long, wet kiss. Picked me up. Backed me up against the garage wall."

"And headed south."

"I haven't been to the south for a long time." Her voice went soft and dreamy, and both of them snorted with laughter. "Forgot how much fun it is there."

"But he reminded you?"

"Oh, he did." Leslie nodded. "It was…so…hot."

"And then did he ask you to drive?"

"No." Leslie shook her head. "When I kissed him, I told him I needed to get back inside and check on you, but he assured me you were fine. That Donna and Frank keep a close eye on everything. And he…took care of me. And that was that. We walked back inside. He stopped at the bar for a drink. And I found you."

Whitney leaned forward to rest her elbows on the table and push her hair back from her face. "You found me? When you could have been…with him? You guys could have…" She shrugged and held her hands out, palms up.

Leslie shook her head. "It was perfect just the way it was, though. He asked Donna about me."

"And she told him? Even though the parties are discreet?"

"She's his aunt."

"What?" Whitney half-screeched and shook her head slightly like she didn't hear Leslie.

"Donna is his mom's sister."

"So, he lives here."

"No." Leslie picked up her beer and took a healthy drink. "Unfortunately, he doesn't."

Whitney slumped in her chair and pursed her lips.

"But you had dinner with him last night."

"Yes."

"And?"

Lou came back to check on them, and they ordered a basket of fries to share. Leslie spilled the details of the dinner date. And dessert. And then dessert at home. Except she skimped a little on the particulars, suspecting suddenly that maybe Whitney did the same. It was one thing to sit here and tell Whitney that Asher had headed due south that first night, but she found she didn't want to talk about every kiss and every stroke of their hands once they were at Leslie's, together in her bed. It felt too much like giving away something special to her, and as much as she loved Whitney, she realized she wanted to be selfish about Asher.

And if Whitney had ever held back with her about Shawn for the same reasons—they had been together for years and batted the *L* word around like the home run derby in the MLB—Leslie completely, totally understood.

She did tell Whitney about his texts, the kisses that had dropped in on her phone all day long. Whitney had squealed with appropriate delight and excitement, and Leslie left the bar later completely caught up in that lighthearted rush of a serious crush that she'd felt all weekend.

Only when she was home alone did it hit her that Asher was gone, and she would have to wait much too long to see him again. Funny, the way that hurt her heart. A week ago, she had no idea who he was, and now, she was certain she couldn't live without him.

Because she'd had dinner with Asher the night before and because she was out that night with Whitney, her kitchen was spotless, except for the ring of dried coffee in the bottom of the glass pot and the two ceramic mugs she and Asher had used earlier in the morning. With nothing to clean, she tossed her purse and keys on the sofa and padded to her room to change her clothes. Eight felt a little early to get ready for bed, but she had no intention of going anywhere or opening her door to anyone. Besides, she was tired. She and Asher hadn't slept much at all.

Ready for a long night of tossing and turning all alone, she returned to the living room and curled up in the corner of her couch. She eyed her book on the round glass-topped coffee table, but she wouldn't be able to concentrate tonight. Opting for channel surfing, she reached for the TV remote further down the couch and snagged the strap of her purse at the same time.

She found a classic black and white movie on TV. Looked like a cheesy horror movie, which made her think of Asher. She unzipped her purse and pulled her phone out, thrilled to find that he had texted her again. This time there were no emojis. He simply asked if he could call her.

She jumped when her phone rang in her hand and pressed it to her ear immediately.

"Hello?"

"Leslie."

Hearing his voice again sent a shiver up her spine.

"Hey."

"I overdid it, didn't I?" he asked without preamble.

"Overdid what?"

"The kisses."

"Are you kidding me?" She laughed softly. "You can't overdo kissing me."

"I wish I was there with you right now. Kissing you."

"Me, too."

"Three weeks. Think you can squeeze me in on your calendar?"

"I will squeeze you anywhere you want me to," she promised.

"See? And you say you're not sure about phone sex."

"I don't wanna wait three weeks to see you again, Asher."

Her words were met with silence, and Leslie dropped her head back to the sofa cushion. Way to blow it, Leslie. Don't be needy. Guys don't like needy, whiny girls.

When he did finally speak, his voice was small and gruff with emotions she was too afraid to name. "Do you mean that?"

"I do." She held her breath.

"I don't, either, Leslie." He groaned, and this time, Leslie heard his frustration loud and clear. She bit her lip before she could suggest that he not wait three weeks, that he come back now and forget Chicago. They certainly weren't at a place where either of them could dictate each other's moves. "I miss you."

Leslie nibbled on her lip. She didn't believe in love at first sight or instalove, but there was something to that first spark of attraction that could lead to more. She'd felt that first spark the first time she'd seen Asher, and she most definitely hoped they would see each other again when he was back in town.

15

Before meeting Asher, Leslie would have said the older she got, the faster time flew by. Not now. After meeting him, after being with him as she had, waiting for the weeks to crawl by until she could see him again made her feel like a ten-year-old waiting for her July birthday to roll around once school was out for the summer.

Her friends kept her busy the first week. Whitney insisted on a couple of shopping sprees—one to buy new lingerie to spice things up for Shawn and one because she desperately needed new jeans. Leslie kept her mouth shut about the lingerie and Shawn, though she did make a few purchases of her own. But she did question Whitney on the jeans; the woman owned at least ten pairs. Leslie lived in jeans—on the job and most times for everyday casual wear—but she constantly washed her denim, so she had some clean.

She joined Jace and Erin a few nights for all the different Hardin ball games. Summer nights were perfect for baseball, so she had no complaints about cheering the kids on. Except that she missed Asher. She imagined what it would be like if he lived here, and the two of them hung out at ball games or went shopping together. She daydreamed about passing rainy days with him, curled up on the couch for movie marathons. She had wicked, dirty dreams about him at night, and she'd taken to crossing the days off her desk calendar at work each night before she clocked out to go home.

During week two, Jace asked her about the calendar, and when she blushed, he teased her. Thankfully, he hadn't shared her crush—she still refused to say much about Asher —with any of his brothers, but it was bad enough that Jace ribbed her now. She supposed it was nice for him to pick on someone else, since he and Erin were still getting needled about having babies.

Rainy days tended to make her think of Asher more, just because she and Whitney had ventured out to the shower in a downpour. It had stopped raining by the time Leslie had wandered out through the yard and found him by the gate. But the air had still been heavy with the smell of fresh rain when they talked, when he kissed her. The Friday of the second week brought another thunderstorm, and Leslie found it nearly impossible to focus on work.

When her phone buzzed just after lunch time, she grabbed for it and held it for a moment while she searched the schematic on her computer screen for the pulley Jace needed to repair a mower deck. Some parts were easy to find, and some were more difficult, and while a pulley should be relatively easy, this particular schematic was blurry and labeled poorly, so it took her a few minutes to find what she needed. She jotted the part number down on a piece of scrap paper and then drew a line under it and finally let her eyes slide over to look at her phone.

I can't get back next week. I'm so sorry.

The text was like a dodgeball smacking her in the belly and robbing her breath away. For a moment, she tried to convince herself it wasn't from Asher. That she'd opened the wrong thread of messages. But his name was at the top of the screen. The last text before this one was his goodnight from last night. Just one kissy face emoji, and yes, he'd slowed down on those, but he still sent them. They still had phone sex, but he still called through daylight hours, too, to say hi. His voice was still soft and sexy and sweet, and Leslie had believed to the bottom of her heart that he was coming back, and they were going to see each other.

She hadn't made any wedding plans, no daydreaming about a shower at his aunt's house. But she'd felt connected to him in a way that was new to her, and she'd thought he felt it, too. This text felt a little cold. Even if he did say I'm sorry. Why couldn't he get back next week? Why wouldn't he explain that to her?

Maybe he'll call, she decided. Her heart didn't feel any better—probably because her brain didn't believe it, either—but she put her phone down gently and turned back to the computer. She'd get busy, and time would fly by, and then he'd call and explain to her what was going on. Probably work. Although, if he had just taken on a new assignment, wouldn't he just call her and tell her that? Or wouldn't he at least have said I'm writing about sheep farms in rural America, so I'll be back after I travel the country? Or maybe he had taken some sexy assignment about wineries in France or Italy, and he would be gone for a long time. Maybe he felt bad that he would be gone for a while, so he didn't want to go into the details now. On the other hand, the Asher she'd slept with, the Asher she'd been talking to and flirting with for the past two weeks, would text and ask her to go with him.

The day after he had left, he'd asked her to join him in a Chicago suburb because he was doing an article on some big anniversary of a town festival. She'd laughed him off, and though he'd laughed, too, his invitation had sounded sincere.

He'd talked about having her at his place in Chicago, too. And she'd blown that suggestion off. Much, much too soon to consider anything of the sort, but if she wanted to, she could take time off and travel with him. Not to France or Italy. Not now. But a Chicago suburb was totally doable.

Asher had promised her he wasn't the kind of guy to hook up with random women, but that didn't mean he wasn't the kind of guy who wanted or needed a woman at home to keep his bed warm. Maybe someone else had turned his head already. And maybe those things he'd said to her the night they were together were just a bunch of lies, things people say to each other in the heat of the moment.

Leslie itched to pick up her phone again, but she wouldn't find anything new. It hadn't buzzed to indicate another text or a voicemail. And she hadn't missed any words in the text. It was hard to read tone or sincerity in a text or email, sure, but staring at it all day wasn't going to make her feel any better.

"Did you find that part?"

She jumped when the shop door swung open and Jace's voice preceded him in. Still caught up in the questions about Asher, she stared at him silently for a second and finally nodded.

"Yeah." She shoved the paper at him when he approached the counter. "It's not a common part. We'll have to order it, and they don't have it in the usual warehouses, so shipping's gonna take a couple of days."

"It's an older mower," he mumbled as he moved behind the counter to study her computer screen. The schematic was still there; Leslie wondered how long she'd been sitting there thinking about Asher. "Okay. I'll call Mr. White and see what he wants to do."

She nodded. Jace, still leaning over her to see her screen, glanced down when her phone buzzed again.

Maybe September.

She didn't pick it up, but she could see the words anyway. Heart in her throat, she dropped her hands to her lap and crossed her fingers out of Jace's sight. If he asked if she was okay now, odds were, she would lose it. Working with a bunch of guys kept her in check, and she rarely had emotional outbursts. In fact, the last had been nearly two years ago, when her grandpa had been sick.

September? Seriously? It was mid-June now. Why bother texting? Why not just let things cool off gradually?

"Wanna do lunch?" Jace asked as he backed away from her. He knew something was up, and she was grateful he was tiptoeing around her emotions. Not that he would be any more comfortable with her having a breakdown than she would.

"No. Thanks. I might work through lunch and leave at four." Her voice sounded normal, steady. She offered him a hopeful smile. Having lunch with Jace would be awkward, because they would both be dancing around that text message, and if he'd seen that one, he'd seen the one above it. And Asher's name at the top of the screen. She didn't want to talk to Jace about Asher; but sitting somewhere with him to eat and not talking about what he'd seen would be just as weird.

She needed Whitney.

"Sure." He nodded. "But are you hungry? I can grab something for you."

She laughed softly as he took another step back toward the shop door. The only thing she wanted at the moment was a drink. That or chocolate. Lots of it.

"I'm good, but thanks."

When Jace left and the coast was clear, Leslie picked up her phone again. She nibbled on her lip as she reread the last two texts from Asher. She wondered if she was supposed to answer him. What was the protocol for being dumped by text? Because she was ninety-nine percent sure he was dumping her.

She tapped the home button so she could send Whitney a message.

Busy to–

She froze when another text from Asher dropped in.

Les? Are you there? Are you upset?

Maybe he didn't know the rules, either. If you dump someone by text, it really wasn't necessary to send follow up messages. No need to beat a dead horse. Or maybe a dead heart, she decided. She reminded herself she had been all in the night he stayed at her house. No matter what the next day brought, she had decided she wanted one night with him, and she wouldn't allow him to hurt her. She wouldn't allow herself to be vulnerable.

It was different, though. He'd said things to her that night, and her stupid, traitorous heart had listened and believed him. And they'd spent hours on the phone since then, sharing not just sex but details about their days, stories from their pasts. Asher had told her he wanted to travel the world; the first big stop on his list was Moscow. Not for work. He'd been to Europe a few times for articles he'd written, but he wanted to go back and live it up in Paris and Venice and Dublin. Leslie had never thought outside the country, but when she'd laughed and said she thought Nashville sounded fun, he'd told her to plan it and they would go.

And now this.

I'm here. Looking up a part for one of my techs.

She could stretch the truth a bit.

The one you dated? That kissed you?

We've come a long way from trying to date and failing at a goodnight kiss.

I'm sorry. About all this stuff coming up.

Stuff. Leslie winced. Stuff was a totally generic word that could mean something had come up or he was just ready to move on. Did he really think she was going to comment? What was she supposed to say to that?

She tapped out of that thread again to text Whitney.

Busy tonight?

Whitney's answer was immediate.

Nope. What's up?

Drinks?

Lou's?

She couldn't do Lou's. This felt too personal, and Lou's was too public.

My house. I'll order pizza.

She wasn't surprised when her phone lit up with a call from her friend.

"Hey." She cleared her throat and looked around the retail space, relieved that she was still alone.

"What did he do?" Whitney asked by way of greeting.

Leslie drew in a deep breath. Phone at her ear, she felt it buzz again and wondered if Asher had texted again.

"Can we just save that for later?"

"Asher?" Whitney's voice jumped an octave. "Really? It is about him?"

"I'm working through lunch." Leslie spoke slowly, working to remain calm. "Leaving at four."

"I'll be there."

"Thanks."

She tossed her phone down, but she couldn't not look at it. She'd missed a call. Asher. Before she could decide what to do, he texted again.

Leslie. Why didn't you answer your phone?

Feeling like a teenager reading a note under her desk in algebra, Leslie stared at her phone, heart in her throat.

I was talking. Making plans for tonight.

Purposely ambiguous. Now she really felt like a brat.

Her phone lit up again. It would be worse to ignore him, but she wanted to. At least for now.

"Hey." Again, she was surprised to sound normal.

"Plans? For tonight?"

"Yeah. I was talking to—"

"Jace? That guy you work with?"

"No. I was talking to Whitney."

"Damn."

"What?" She took a deep breath and let it out as quietly as possible. Because she'd just wasted at least a half hour of company time, she propped her phone in the crook of her neck and pulled her keyboard closer. She'd get started on the parts order, though she didn't have to send it for another couple of hours.

"You sounded the alarm. Already?"

She knew exactly what he meant, but she had no desire to get into this conversation while she was at work.

"Asher, Whit and I are together all the time."

"You're mad."

"No, I'm not. Disappointed, but not mad."

"I was going to call you. Tonight. Explain everything."

That sounded so ominous, Leslie actually shivered.

"Asher, it's fine," she insisted, because if by explain everything he meant let her down easy, she wasn't interested.

"Fine," he repeated. "Fine. When a woman says fine, it's not fine."

She sighed and ducked her head to rub the back of her neck.

"September?" she whispered. "Why such a long time?"

She mentally cursed herself for giving in and steeled herself for whatever lies he pulled from his sleeve.

"Part of it's work," he hedged. "I just ducked out of a

meeting to call you. I gotta get back in there. I'll call you tonight."

"Okay."

Felt like another blow off, and again, Leslie wondered why he wouldn't just let it go. But she didn't want to continue the conversation here, anyway.

"Will you still wait for me?" he asked quietly.

Because she wasn't sure at the moment that she trusted him, and because she was at work and losing control of her emotions, she wouldn't answer him.

"I gotta go, Asher. I'll talk to you later."

She clicked off before he could respond, and then she sat in the everyday quiet of her work space that suddenly felt louder and more profound than ever before. She and Asher hadn't had a chance to date. Not really. One dinner date. And some skin-to-skin contact that had been mutually satisfying.

But that phone call sure felt like a break up call.

Again feeling like a mopey teenager, Leslie dropped her phone in her purse, zipped the bag closed, and returned her attention to her work.

She didn't take her phone from her purse again until after four when she said a quick goodbye to Jace and darted out in the rain to her Rav 4. She wasn't sure what to expect when she unzipped her purse for a peek at her phone, but the hollow in her belly when she found nothing new on the screen was impossible to deny.

Once at home, she changed into sporty shorts and a t-shirt and twisted the top off a longneck bottle. Whitney arrived just after five, a twelve-pack in hand. Leslie was torn between laughing and crying when she saw it. They ordered pizza and then collapsed to opposite ends of the couch to commiserate. Things were back to status quo for Whitney and Shawn, which didn't mean happy, but Whitney always seemed to settle. Leslie was happy to listen to Whitney, though, because now that the time had come to spill the beans on Asher, she didn't want to. Not that she wanted to shield him from her overprotective best friend. She just didn't want to wallow, and if she started talking about him, she was going to wallow.

"So." Whitney nudged Leslie's leg with her foot. "What's going on? You're down to a week left on your countdown."

"A week and two months, maybe."

"What?"

"He texted me today. And said next week wasn't going to work out. When I didn't answer, he texted again and said maybe September."

"September? As in July, August, September?"

Leslie nodded, her throat a little tight now.

"And why the change in his schedule?"

"I don't know. He called when you and I were talking. Then he called again. Said he was gonna call later."

"Oh, I've heard that one before." Whitney raised her eyebrows.

"I know."

"Do you believe him? That he was going to call?"

"I honestly don't know, Whit. I don't know if I wanna talk to him."

"You don't want an explanation?"

Leslie shrugged dramatically. "What if he's just going to lie? And then come September, he puts me off again for reasons that sound believable?"

"What if it's work? Or something else he has no control over?"

"Why not just let it go?"

"What if he had every intention of being here next week and he just can't?"

"Why not call me? And talk to me? Who does that by text?"

"He said he was going to call you."

"After he knew I was upset."

"You told him?"

"I told him I was talking to you on the phone."

That made Whitney chuckle. "Oh. So, he was upset because you sounded the alarm and called your girlfriend."

"I just don't want to play games, Whit."

"You'd have handed Shawn his walking papers years ago, if you were me. Am I right?"

"Yep." Leslie nodded. "And you'd give Asher the benefit of the doubt here. Am I right?"

Whitney winced and nodded.

"You should hear him out."

"I told myself I could do this." Leslie brushed at her eyes, irritated by her tears. "That I could have a fling. Appreciate it for what it was and let it go."

"Flings don't last two weeks."

Leslie rolled her eyes. "Please. I dated my high school boyfriend longer. And we were freshmen."

The doorbell rang, but Leslie let Whitney answer it. She listened from the couch while her friend flirted with the pizza guy and then sat up straight to laugh about it when Whitney carried the box to the sofa.

"I'll grab napkins," she said as she climbed to her feet. She hustled to the kitchen to grab napkins and paper plates. She handed all of it to Whitney and then went back for another beer for both of them.

"What if he found someone else?" Leslie asked when she plopped back down by Whitney.

"What if…his place was robbed and he's dealing with insurance stuff?"

"God, please tell me you didn't believe Shawn if he fed you that line."

Whitney snorted. "He didn't. I wouldn't. I just...Les, you're crazy about this guy."

"Maybe I just got carried away because of the incredible sex."

Whitney sighed. "Maybe. But I think you owe it to him to hear him out."

"If he calls." Leslie glanced at her phone, sitting silently on the coffee table.

"He will. It's early. He knew you were hanging out with me."

"He asked if I was with Jace."

Whitney laughed, but she tipped her head. "He's jealous."

"Which means nothing."

Later, after most of the pizza was gone, and they'd watched several episodes of *Friends*, Leslie caught Whitney texting Shawn and sent her home. Whitney tried to argue, but Leslie insisted she go be with Shawn. After stacking the paper plates inside the pizza box and carrying their empty bottles to the kitchen, Whitney finally gave in and reached for her purse and her keys.

"Call me," she said simply, and Leslie nodded.

When eleven o'clock rolled around and Asher still hadn't called, Leslie turned off the TV and the lights and went to bed. Angry with herself for being hurt about Asher, she tossed her phone down on the nightstand, turned her lamp off, and pulled her comforter over her head.

And refused to let her mind wander to thoughts of Asher. Here. In her bed. With her.

16

She was dreaming of Asher, of making love to him in a thunderstorm, when she awoke to the sounds of tapping and vibrating. Leslie lay flat on her back for a moment in her dark bedroom trying to pull herself together. The first thing she was aware of when she finally blinked the last of the sexy dreams away was the time. It was after one in the morning, and he hadn't called. She rolled over to her side and squeezed her eyes closed again, only to hear the tapping again.

In her dream, that sound had been hail.

Maybe it was storming again. The rain had let up a bit earlier after she got home, but another storm had rolled in not long after Whitney had arrived. The vibrating noise started again. Leslie turned over and reached out in the darkness to turn her lamp on. Her phone jumped on the nightstand, but as she started to pick it up, she heard a loud pounding noise outside.

Maybe she was still sleeping. Maybe her dreams of making love with Asher had turned darker, and now she was bordering on nightmare mode. She flipped her phone over to see who was calling, not surprised and trying not to be thrilled when she saw that it was him calling.

"Hello?"

She wanted to give him hell. First for not calling earlier, when she'd been waiting to hear from him and for calling now, when she had been sleeping and dreaming of him. But she didn't. She barely pushed the whispered greeting through her lips, and then she huddled into her pillow waiting for him to speak. What if he was drunk? Not that she'd ever seen him lose control, but why else would he wait until an ungodly hour like this to call her and explain about the *stuff* that was going to keep him away until September?

"Leslie."

"Yes."

"Are you home?"

Leslie rolled her eyes and shook her head. Was he seriously going to start playing the jealousy card now?

"Will you let me in?"

"What?"

"I'm at your front door. Will you let me in?"

"You're—?" She sat up in bed, but her brain was still sleep-fogged, because she thought he said he was at her front door. Maybe she was still dreaming. She wanted to see him so badly, her brain was going to play this out for her. This time they were going to make love in her bed rather than outside in a thunderstorm.

"I've been calling you and knocking on your door. Will you let me in?"

"Why didn't you ring the doorbell?"

As if that mattered. She almost asked why he was here, how he was here, but odds were he was getting rained on. The stoop out front had a tiny aluminum covering, and it sounded like the wind was whipping the rain around sideways again.

She padded out of her room and to the door, but once there, she hesitated. Hoping he wouldn't notice, she tiptoed over to the bay window and peeked out through the blinds to see his truck in her drive.

"What're you doing here?" She whispered the words into her phone as she yanked open the door to let him in. His ponytail looked a bit longer than when she last saw him, and his eyes were bloodshot, but Asher had never looked better to her.

"Can I come in?" He propped his hands on the frame of the door and leaned in toward her.

"Yes." She stepped back to give him room. Cold rainwater dripped on her bare toes when he came inside. "Asher. What's going on?"

He closed the door and then toed off his worn, wet loafers.

"You sounded the alarm, babe," he reminded her. "I thought about calling you, and I figured you and Whitney already had me set to hang, so I finished what business I could and got in my car and hauled ass down here."

"Set to hang? What?" She rubbed her eyes, her phone still in her hand.

"Tell me you've saved your beautiful face and pussy for me." He cupped her chin in his hand and forced her to look him in the eyes.

"I have." She nodded.

He lowered his face to hers and pressed his lips over hers in a scorching kiss she felt down to her toes. Leslie's hands moved without her permission. She tossed her phone in the direction of the recliner and reached for him. Her fingers roamed over his face, hungry for the feel of his skin. He was chilled from the storm; she combed her fingers back around his neck and tugged the elastic from his hair.

"You're wet." She kissed a trail from his lips to his ear, tasting the rain on his skin.

"Are you?"

He molded his hands over her upper arms as Leslie played with his hair. She nodded in response when he nuzzled her neck and then nipped at her shoulder blade.

"Why don't you find out?" she suggested, moving her arms, sinking her hands into his broad, strong shoulders.

Rather than answer her, Asher gathered the hem of her oversized sleepshirt in his hands and lifted it up over her head. Topless and chilled before him, her nipples grew hard and goosebumps pebbled her skin. Asher's cold hands cupped the curves of her breasts. Leslie, desperate to feel him, tugged anxiously at his belt buckle. He didn't help her, and her hands shook with both pleasure—he played with her nipples—and need as she fought to undress him. Jeans open at his waist, Leslie turned her attention to his shirt and shoved it up over his chest. To remove it, she had to step closer to him, and Asher wound his arms around her when she pushed up on her tiptoes to pull the shirt over his head. His chest was warm and solid, and Leslie closed her eyes and pressed her face to his neck. She was thrilled to be in his arms again, and she refused to wonder what his sudden appearance meant.

Asher plunged his hands inside her panties and cupped her ass cheeks with a hungry squeeze. She wiggled to help him when he pushed them low over her hips. Within seconds, the lace was on the floor, Asher lifted her, and she wrapped her legs around his waist. Rather than head for the bedroom, Asher crossed the room in a few big steps and pressed her against the wall. She didn't comment when he tugged his wallet from his pocket and fished a condom out.

"For you," he told her as he tore it open. Leslie pushed his jeans down and freed his cock from his briefs. The sight of his strong hands rolling the rubber over his cock made her ache for him, and finally, he looked up at her and met her gaze.

She nodded, but when he stroked his thumb over her clit and into her folds, she dropped her head back to the wall and closed her eyes.

"Hang on, babe." His voice was low, tight with coiled emotion, ready to be unleashed. She cried out when he drove into her, but the pressure, his power, was delicious. He pounded her against the wall hard enough to rattle a picture frame but not hard enough to break her.

She chanted to him, begging him not to stop. Her hands roamed his bare back and pulled his hair, and her tongue tasted the rain and the five o'clock shadow on his face. When a wave of warmth climbed her lower legs, she moaned softly and whispered to him that she was close. Rather than rush it, Asher slowed his thrusts down, careful to drag his cock over every sensitive bit of her body between her legs. When he finally drew his name from her lips in a harsh shout, he drove home one more time and bucked against her. He ducked his head to her shoulder to catch his breath; Leslie smoothed her hands over his hair and kissed the side of his head.

"What are you doing here?" she whispered when their strangled breathing settled and the house was quiet enough to hear the rain again.

"You were ready to give up." He lifted his head to look her in the eye. "Today. You were ready to walk away. I'm not gonna let that happen."

"Asher."

"No." He shook his head. "Don't tell me I'm wrong. One text, and you were ready to let us go."

Leslie licked her lips and smoothed her fingertips over his cheekbone.

"But that text, Asher." She frowned and shook her head. "I mean...to just announce that next week wasn't going to work."

"I know."

"And then say *maybe September*?" She sighed. "What was I supposed to think?"

"You thought I was blowing you off."

She shrugged, but she eventually nodded.

"I was going to call. I was just frustrated with my situation, and I couldn't call you at that second. And so, I texted, and it was a douche thing to do, and I'm sorry."

"If you find someone else, just tell me, Asher. Don't lie or put me off."

"There's no one else. Leslie, it's just you. Remember when I asked if you believed in love at first sight?"

"Of course." She pressed her thumb to the center of his lips and nodded. "I remember every second we've been together."

"You didn't ask me."

"Ask you what?"

"If I do. Believe in love at first sight."

Leslie drew in a quick breath, surprised by his words.

"Do you?"

"I didn't." He shook his head. "Until you."

"Asher—"

"Can I stay?"

"What?"

"Tonight? Can I stay? Or are you going to kick me out?"

"Stay." She barely whispered the word, but she could see that in the silence, he heard her clearly. Legs still wrapped around his waist, Leslie buried her face in his neck when he kicked out of his jeans and briefs and carried her to the bedroom.

"*Life Journey* offered me an article I couldn't pass up," he told her as he set her on her bed.

She reached for him as she fell back on her pillow. Seemed like she'd heard of the magazine, but she couldn't be sure. After the scene in the living room, she was likely to believe anything he told her.

"It's a non-denominational...spiritual life...kind of publication."

Leslie laughed softly as he slipped his fingers between her legs.

"And you've got your fingers inside me as you tell me about it."

"Sex with you is a beautiful thing." He kissed her forehead. "I've written for them before. Wrote about the pros and cons of meditation and yoga practices. The pay is excellent. So. There's a kid...he's from some armpit-hole-in-the-wall town in Washington."

"The state?"

"Yes." Asher moved his hand now and stroked the sensitive skin along her inner thigh. Leslie closed her eyes. "The kid was raised in some sort of cult, but he got away. Some family member took him back, but the cult leaders were pissed and came looking for him. It was a big deal, but it was such a tiny, weird little cult and such a small town, not much about it made national news. The kid killed his brother, so now he's in prison. But he's found salvation or something. *Life Journey* wants me to write a human-interest piece on it, and there's been talk about a book."

"Oh. Wow."

"I'll have to spend a lot of time there," he said quietly.

"I get it."

"Do you?"

The lamp was still on from when Leslie had turned it on earlier, so she saw the concern etched into the skin around his eyes.

"Yes."

"I want the article. I want the book."

She nodded. "I wouldn't want you to pass on that for me."

"Why do I have to choose, Leslie?" he asked softly. "When I texted you earlier, and again, I'm sorry for how I handled that...I was with my dad. He was with his oncologist."

She winced.

"It's okay. But he's gonna start chemo next week, and that's why I needed to wait to come back home."

"I'm so sorry," she whispered.

"Dad's a fighter," Asher said simply. "But I want to be part of his fight."

"Okay."

"I also spent the afternoon on the phone with friends to find someone to sublease my damned apartment in the city."

"For when you're in Washington."

"Forever," he corrected her. "Because even though I plan to be part of Dad's fight, I plan to be a resident here in Rockfield. I know it's too soon to suggest living together, and I won't live with Donna and Frank, but there are some interesting old homes here with some good bones. Good foundations."

"What're you saying?"

Asher shifted to lie between her thighs and press a kiss to her lips.

"If I'm a freelance writer, home base is anywhere I choose to be."

Leslie's eyes burned, but she blinked the tears away.

"And I choose to be somewhere close to you."

"I gave that whole love at first sight thing some thought." She cleared her throat and took a deep breath.

"Yeah?" He cocked an eyebrow.

"And while I'm not sure you can fall in love instantly like that...I think you can feel a spark."

"I feel lots of sparks when I'm with you." He pressed a kiss to the underside of her chin.

She smiled and then wiggled when he slipped his hands between their bodies to stroke her breasts.

"And that spark can either vanish instantly or catch fire. I felt a spark...the first time I saw you."

"And?"

"I'm on fire, Asher," she whispered.

"Are you okay with me finding a place here? To be closer to you?"

"Yes."

"Will you trust me? When I have to travel for work?"

"Yes."

"Will you go with me? If I ever write about something exciting?"

"You don't have to write anything exciting, Asher. Being with you is enough to take my breath away."

"Leslie?"

"Hmm?"

Asher inched back over her belly.

"Do you work on Saturdays?"

"Hardin Landscaping is closed on Saturdays."

"So, we have no reason to be up early?"

"Breakfast in bed."

"Which we could do at noon, if we wanted." He arched a brow. "Right?"

She nodded and bent her knees when Asher moved further back on the bed and kissed her belly.

"Or we could just have breakfast right now." He dragged his teeth over her inner thigh and then flicked her clit with his tongue. "And then again later."

"When we get up."

"Oh, I'm up, Leslie Brewer. I am always up for you."

SNEAK PEEK AT KISS & MAKE UP,
STORY #2

Whitney Oliver heard the muted singular ring of her desk phone, but she didn't look. She couldn't. She couldn't tear her eyes away from her cell phone—the one she really shouldn't have out of her purse right now, while she was at work. Her brain had gone into overdrive when she saw the photo plastered all over Shawn Green's social media. He hadn't posted it, no, but *still*. The dark-haired chick with the nose ring and the spiked hair had tagged him in the picture, and besides, it was him *in* the photo, so he couldn't say he didn't know, it wasn't him, blah blah blah.

Okay, so the chick had clothes on. Sort of. If you counted that skimpy little black tank bra as a top. Whitney didn't. The picture was just from the waist up, so she couldn't see what else the chick had on. What she could see was that she had no tits, but she was either cold that night in Texas at the ball game—Whitney had never been to a Rangers game on a June evening, so she couldn't say if the girl should be cold—or she was pretty into Shawn Green.

The hell of it? If Whitney brought it up now? He would remind her that they broke up *before* he left for Texas on a boys' trip. He could also say that nothing happened, that he and his friends just hung out with some girls at the game, no big. He *had* said that. A few times now. He could also throw it back at her that she hadn't stayed at home pining away over him when he was gone. That she'd gone to a party with a friend and had some side action. Except that Whitney hadn't really told him that. She'd mentioned that Leslie Brewer had gone with her to a wedding shower, but she hadn't gone into details.

Why now, though? Why—three weeks after the fact—was this chick *just now* posting a picture of some random guy she met in Arlington, Texas and watched a baseball game and ate peanuts with? Was there more to the story? Were they still in contact? Shawn had dropped other names casually—the girls hanging on his buddies that night—but he hadn't mentioned anyone named Kori.

ABOUT THE AUTHOR

TE Sheridan is the author of thirty women's fiction and contemporary romance novels. She lives in the Midwest with her husband and two children.

This is her first published work written under the pen name TE Sheridan.

www.ingramcontent.com/pod-product-compliance
Lightning Source LLC
Chambersburg PA
CBHW020308150626
46552CB00022B/2112